Some Kind of Lonely Clown

The Music, Memory, and Melancholy Lives of Karen Carpenter

Joel Samberg

Published in the USA by:
BearManor Media
P O Box 71426
Albany, Georgia 31708
www.bearmanormedia.com

ISBN: 978-1-59393-868-0
BearManor Media, Albany, Georgia
Printed in the United States of America
Cover image by Stewart Marshall
Book design by Robbie Adkins, www.adkinsconsult.com

To my wife Bonnie,
whose inspiration, love, and support never waver,
no matter *what* I'm listening to.

Acknowledgements

Karen Carpenter, the instantly recognizable voice of the Carpenters, touched many lives through her music, her personality and individuality, and her need to be in love. There are many people who willingly shared and discussed their thoughts and recollections with me, and they are acknowledged below. There are also many who chose *not* to share and discuss their thoughts and recollections; all these years later, memories and emotions remain heartrending for them, and that's why they decided not to take this voyage with me. I wish they had, but respect their decision not to. What's more, there is a certain amount of loyalty and dedication—related to the early days and the heydays—that, for one reason or another, prompted some people to avoid exposing any truths or feelings at all. These people, too, are mostly absent from these pages. Still, there are plenty of coworkers and acquaintances out there who willingly and eagerly agreed to help me explore the topic and share some stories that add value to the journey and support some of the interpretations therein. There are also plenty of modern-day devotees and professional observers who were instrumental in providing various ideas, shapes, colors, and moods to this special project, some who have already walked a similar path journalistically, and others who have used their own talents for impressive legacy-related projects of their own. Finally, there is a group of relatives and friends who stood behind me, as they do for all my literary efforts, even when they're not entirely thrilled to be standing next to me when I ask them to look at or listen to certain things.

The only task harder than putting a deadline on the effort to track down all the people I wanted to track down is deciding in what order to acknowledge them, since they were all so valuable to my research and deserving of my deepest thanks. So I'll take the easy way out. I'll do it alphabetically, except for the first few, who all worked at A&M Records at one time or another.

These A&M employees came aboard to provide anecdotes, angles and points of view, and I'm thrilled that they did: Doug Haverty, Jon Konjoyan, Ronny Schiff (from Almo, the music publishing arm), and Thomas Vicari.

Gary Alt is a friend, musician and radio host (on WNTI, Hackettstown, New Jersey) who helps me out on projects, etymologically, technologically, and in other ways, more times than he probably cares to realize (because realizing it only ages us both). He even once played a Carpenters song on his radio show, as a present to me, even though his radio show was devoted the Beatles.

I was honored to have made the acquaintance of Carolyn Arzac, a close friend of Karen Carpenter's secretary, Evelyn Wallace, who graciously provided stories she fondly remembers and photos she had the prudence to shoot.

Michael Bingham, the editor of *New Haven Magazine*, accepted one of my first journalistic forays into the world of Karen, which, in turn, led to more research, fascination and, ultimately, this book.

Legendary Wrecking Crew and Carpenters session drummer Hal Blaine spoke to me about those days as if they were only yesterday.

Michelle Berting Brett, who sings beautifully in the tribute show, *We've Only Just Begun*, and her husband, Mark, who produces it, submitted to interviews and email chats after we became friends at a show they put on at Bridge Street Live in Collinsville, CT.

My buddy from high school, Bob Buono, whom I met two years after I got slammed against a locker (which will be discussed later), never slammed me against anything because he supports me no matter what crazy scheme I get involved with. He, too, likes the Carpenters, though not as much as he likes Maynard Ferguson.

Drummer Liberty DeVitto, who worked on Karen's solo album, sent me a couple of great stories and provided a few considered opinions.

New York song stylist Barbara Fasano, a friend from Hofstra University, agreed to give me some perspective on what a professional singer takes away from the experience of hearing Karen's instrument. Also from Hofstra, Marc Feingold was a constant source of inspiration by making me laugh and realize that as long as we're both giving it the old college try, anything is possible. Our mutual friend, musician Mindye Fortgang, who made believe she broke her arm during the opening performance of Hempstead Teen Repertory's *Snow White Goes West* (in which I played Hank), also provided a professional perspective on the musical gift of Karen.

Carl Goldman, a radio host in Los Angeles during the active Carpenter years and current owner of KHTS-AM, Santa Clarita, CA, shared some thoughts on his very special interview with Karen.

Rick Henry, an incredibly devoted and talented fan, who keeps several online efforts safely humming along and spearheads other projects to keep the legacy alive and kicking, provided several important comments and recommendations.

A long-distance thank you to the managing editor and editor of *Metropolis*, Martin Keroux and Michael Kanert, respectively. *Metropolis* is the largest English-language magazine in Japan. I tapped into Martin and Michael for their points of view on the Carpenters' enduring popularity over there.

Felice Mancini, who gave the Carpenters the lyric to one of their simplest and most elegant songs, was equally simple and elegant in her recollections.

Stewart Marshall, a gifted digital-photo artist from England, provided some of his digital-photo artwork for this book, including the cover image. Stewart manipulates photos using lights, colors, and textures to create interpretive pieces of art. He has done similar work for images from *Star Wars* and of Elvis Presley, but calls Karen his favorite study.

Chris May deserves an extra special mention because he's been an extra special supporter of this project. His role as an arranger, musicologist, and record industry aficionado came in extremely handy, as did his archived radio interviews (collectively called "The Download") with several key figures from the story.

Dr. Amy Nulsen, Ph.D., joins the chorus of many who note that the first time they heard anorexia nervosa discussed in public was shortly after Karen passed away (she deals with the disorder as part of her practice). When Dr. Nulsen learned that I was writing this book, she accepted my invitation to discuss it from both a professional and personal point of view, and I thank her for that.

There might not have been a book at all if not for the encouragement and backing of the brave and visionary Ben Ohmart of BearManor Media (the Herb Alpert of publishing, without the trumpet). I wish tons and tons and tons of success for him (and plenty of health and happiness). After all, a lot of success for him means a little for me, too.

Brian Panella, a personal manager in the music business, whose clients have included Peggy Lee, Diahann Carroll, and Tony Sandler, remembers meeting Karen at the 1971 Grammy Awards and shared some interesting showbiz stories with me when he heard about this project.

Eric Pierce, editor of the *Downey Patriot*, gave me a lot of space in his newspaper to write about Karen, with a thematic structure that served as a foundation for my later work.

Emily Rosenthal, MA, LCSW, was gracious enough to take some time out of her busy Manhattan practice, where she specializes in eating disorders, to discuss anorexia nervosa and help me validate some of my own perceptions as they relate to Karen. It didn't hurt that in addition to being an LCSW, Emily is also a BKCF (Big Karen Carpenter Fan).

The entire Samberg clan put up with my fixation to cover this journalistic territory, as well as my obsession to the music that turned it into a fixation in the first place. If they didn't always quite share it with me, they certainly gave me the love, respect, and kind smiles I needed to carry on without turning into a miserable recluse. The supportive clan includes Bonnie Samberg (wife of 34 years—though we've only just begun), Celia and Dave Stangarone, (whose three children, Veronica, Sam, and Jill, put me on top of the world as a grandpa), Kate Samberg and Jim Buffone (thanks, Kate, for remembering to bring back the *Close to You* album cover when you gave up the Brooklyn apartment), and Daniel Samberg (who spent time in Brazil, but just to needle me still refuses to acknowledge how much Brazilians love the Carpenters).

Randy Schmidt's book, *Little Girl Blue: The Life of Karen Carpenter,* is an affectionate and comprehensive portrait that is indispensable for all Karen Carpenter fans, past and present. Randy didn't mind making room on his active calendar as a teacher and author to share some of his thoughts for this book, and his willingness to do so is highly appreciated.

Harry Sharpe was the music director for Donna Summer when she and the Carpenters were inducted into the Hollywood Bowl Hall of Fame. "It was quite a thrill to see Richard's handwritten charts," says Harry, who told me all about meeting Richard and the vibe he got from him during that assignment. Thanks, Harry.

Graham Smith was senior producer on National Public Radio's *All Things Considered* when he accepted my proposal for a story entitled "Remembering Karen Carpenter, 30 Years Later," another project that sparked the creation of this book. Thanks for the spark, Graham.

The late Doug Strawn, who played with the Carpenters for their entire run, spent some valuable time with me on the phone to talk about those very special days. We miss you, Doug.

Singer/songwriter/performer Neil Sedaka is both a legend and a gentleman, and I very much appreciate the recollections he shared with me about the tour he did with the Carpenters in 1975.

Chris Tassin, a Karen devotee of incomparable artistic skill, put aside some time to chat with me about the object of his affection.

Distinguished deejay Charlie Tuna, who sounds as good today as he did back then, responded to my inquiries with the same enthusiasm.

Dr. Gibbs Williams, Ph.D., a noted New York psychoanalyst, author, and educator with more than thirty years of experience, is a client of my corporate copywriting who turned into a Karen fan when I sent him to some online information prior to grilling him for professional comments on her personal issues. He ended up grilling *me* about my fascination. I didn't mind too much.

Pam Zeitler and Tom Kurt of the Florida-based Carpenters Tribute Band were happy to bring the same passion to our interviews that they bring to their live show.

Thank you all.

Table of Contents

Introduction:
Yesterday and Today

"Karen Carpenter sings."

–Page 176 of the 1964 Downey High School yearbook

This is how it all began.

Fall 1971. Two bullies, a skinny one and a chubby one, approached me in the social studies and math wing of William Tresper Clarke Junior & Senior High School, in Westbury, Long Island. Not that it matters, but I think their names were Michael and Randy. They were eighth graders, like me, but a world apart in disposition. They were, after all, bullies.

I suspect that one or both of them must have seen the doodles on the back cover of my notebook: blue ink outlines of an electric guitar and a drum set, probably a trumpet and a saxophone, too, and a microphone for good measure. Either they had noticed those doodles or saw some sheet music sticking out between two textbooks; I had sheet music with me at all times because a few buddies and I were in the process of forming a band of our own, which I wanted to call Long Island Sound (it sounded a lot more clever back then than it does now), and we often discussed arrangements between classes. Anyway, the reason I think that Michael and Randy must have seen the doodles or the sheet music is because after following me down the hallway for a few moments, they suddenly seemed to have music on their collective mind.

"Hey, Samberg," one of them called out, "what's your favorite group?"

Even a relatively clueless red-headed, freckle-faced kid like me knew that Michael and Randy expected to hear something *other* than Black Sabbath, Grand Funk Railroad, Jefferson Airplane, or one of a dozen other rock bands that only their ilk was allowed to listen to. It was a no-win situation for me: if I lied, they'd know it, for I'd have been unable to name a single song or band member of any of those groups, and that would have given Michael and Randy permission to knock the books out from under my arm and kick them down the hall; but if I told the truth and mentioned some of the groups I really *was* listening to at the time, that, too, would have been a license for those two bullies to bully me around.

With such a limited choice, I chose to tell the truth.

"I like the Carpenters," I said, with an inflection designed to let them know that it wasn't the *only* group I listened to—that there were others, as well. But before I could add any to the list, Michael blew out his lips like a donkey and chuckled.

"The Carpenters," he said—not as a question, but a confirmation that I had mentioned one of the groups that he was certain I was going to mention.

"Yes. They have some neat stuff," I added confidently, "and their arrangements are kind of interesting."

But the two of them had no interest in whatever I was going to say to defend my choice. It was time for them to wrap it up. There were other kids to pick on. So they slammed me against the locker, then walked away laughing.

Skip ahead to 2009. My twenty-two-year-old daughter Kate, who was moving into her first apartment, asked if she could look through my old record collection to select a few album covers to frame and use as wall decorations. Apparently that was a bit of a trend for first apartments at the time. So, I took her into the basement of my home, where I had about seventy-five albums, most of which fit into a time period roughly between 1965 and 1983. She flipped through, grabbed the *Rubber Soul* album by the Beatles, *American Pie* by Don McLean, and *Close to You*, the one and only album by the Carpenters that I had ever purchased. That was back in late 1970. I was thirteen at the time. Before Kate took it away, I glanced at the picture on the cover: there was Karen Carpenter, in a billowy white dress, next to her brother, Richard, wearing an open jacket and sporting a Prince Valiant haircut, both of them sitting on a large rock by a bay. Identical smiles. They looked as if someone had told them to say "cheese" at the count of three. I don't recall what, if anything, I thought about the cover image back then, but now, if prompted to give an impulsive critical assessment, the phrase 'ill at ease' might suffice.

During the Michael and Randy days, I was aware only of perhaps a dozen-and-a-half Carpenters songs in all—the twelve on the *Close to You* album, which included two enormous hits, "(They Long to Be) Close to You" and "We've Only Just Begun," and a few of their follow-up hit singles. Among those were "For All We Know," "Rainy Days and Mondays," and "Superstar." I doubt I gave the *Close to You* album more than a half-dozen spins in its entirety, which for a fairly busy junior high school kid was still a significant investment in time. After those half-dozen spins, other musical interests took over—interests that I was able to share with my friends. Truth be told, that had not really been the case with the Carpenters.

There were plenty of musical choices to select from in my local record store, fueled by what I heard on AM radio: Three Dog Night, John Denver, Carole King, George Harrison, Carly Simon, America, Simon & Garfunkel, Creedence Clearwater Revival, Aretha Franklin, Bread, James Taylor, and dozens of others. But since I never had enough money to buy as many albums as I would have liked, I limited my purchases to a just a few, and that Carpenters album had been one of them. So obviously there was *something* about them that prompted me to make the investment.

I gave Kate the album cover and, out of curiosity, took the actual 33-rpm disc upstairs to listen to it once again, but my ancient record player didn't have a needle anymore and I hadn't bothered to shop for a new one since Kate was in kindergarten, sixteen years earlier.

So, I borrowed the *Close to You* CD from the library to reacquaint myself with the album. What I heard, and what I began to remember from the old days, were lots of overdubbed *ooohs* and *wahhhhs*; more oboes, French horns, and harps than I was used to hearing in pop music over the years; lightweight yet hummable songs of loves lost and found, about good feelings and bad bosses; some original compositions and some borrowed from Bacharach and David, Williams and Nichols, Lennon and McCartney; not rock, not jazz, but not a hundred percent middle-of-the-road, either, because of the complexity of many of the orchestrations; and Karen's voice, of course—that plaintive and formidable contralto for which she became, like the title of the Carpenters' fifth hit single, a superstar.

I began to wonder what else was in the Carpenters' catalog that I had missed, having owned just that one album. So, I visited the Internet, particularly YouTube, and discovered that despite what some detractors might wish to believe, the Carpenters' overall song output cannot easily be categorized. There are just too many categories.

Suddenly I was faced with a group I didn't really know at all.

Like many others, I already knew that Karen had died young, and that her death had been attributed to the damage caused by the condition known as anorexia nervosa. I had always assumed that after she was gone, her brother Richard was simply unable to ride the wave of pop magic that he had conjured up so successfully with his sister. As I continued to explore their history, I began to realize there was a lot more to the Carpenters' story than just their music. I came to learn that Karen was an extremely troubled soul, that she may have had serious inherent issues that were only made more difficult by having to deal with a stern and emotionally detached mother, an ambitious and hard-driven brother, and the effects of being thrust under a global spotlight at just twenty years of age. The childlike world she loved—all iced tea and Disney characters—was not the dauntingly grown-up world in which she was compelled to live.

Little by little, I came to see that the popularity of the Carpenters in general, and Karen in particular, has never really waned, and that in some respects it has even grown to the point where it might be said that there's been a Carpenters revival brewing for several years now. There are many tribute bands currently touring the U.S. and abroad; there is an abundance of active websites (and Facebook pages) devoted to Karen's legacy; there are hundreds of social media sites that discuss, debate, and praise Karen, and countless YouTube music videos that feature thousands of posted comments from fans who are effusive in their love and longing for what they consider to be Karen's gift:

"It's the sound of heaven."

"I miss you so much, Karen, and you just know there are tears in my eyes as I write this."

"Definitely the best vocalist I've ever heard. No one can sing with such an angelic and unique voice."

"A more soothing and tender voice there will never be."

"Her voice is comfort, like being wrapped in a warm blanket."

I doubt any of this would sway Michael and Randy, but it made me even more curious, and for that I am grateful to the two bullies and the locker they slammed me against.

As my journey continued, I sensed that there were dozens of stories within and behind the ones that have already been published, and hundreds of unanswered questions. I also came to believe that there were many different Karens. We were already familiar with the gifted singer and consummate recording artist, but we must not forget the love-starved romantic, the trusting prey, the obedient daughter, the conflicted sister, the awkward performer, the unpredictable jester, the modest millionaire, the optimistic dreamer, the wannabe mother, the emotional wreck, the fleeting liar, the giddy clown, the generous friend. Nor must we overlook the ailing anorexic and doomed icon.

This curious 'List of Karens' is not simply an exercise in whimsical rhetoric but, in a way, can almost be considered a literal reality: between 1970 and 1982 there were thousands of photographs taken, dozens of promotional videos produced, and countless media profiles published about the Carpenters, and scrutinizing just a fraction of them brings to light the fact that Karen's looks, style, mannerisms, expressions, performance techniques, perhaps even her personality and attitudes seemed to have changed more times in twelve years than most of us change resumes in thirty. How can all those changes *not* be a consequence of the existence of so many Karens? She was almost thespian in the way her appearance, manner, and character transformed from performance to performance, video to video, year to year. In one YouTube clip, for example, she might seem like an 'aw shucks' country gal, in the next, a sullen waif, and in the next a naive temptress. Those who assert that acting on stage and screen would have been her salvation into self-confidence and fulfillment have a good case for saying so simply because of her chameleon-like disposition.

In one respect, it is perfectly understandable. After all, most people do modify the way they look and act from time to time, and coming of age as Karen did in the early 1970s could not have been easy for anyone, let alone a nobody who became an internationally-famous somebody before her twenty-first birthday.

Then, of course, there was the anorexia—which may, of course, have something to do with that chameleon-like disposition, according to the psychiatric professionals with whom I consulted. Emily Rosenthal, a New York-based psychotherapist, who treats people with eating disorders, says that people who suffer from the disorder are among the truest actors around. "They are often highly sensitive, attuned to others' needs, preferences, vulnerabilities, and desires, and prioritize others' approval over their own internal cues and authentic selves," she explains. "This can make relationships and interactions performance-like, geared to an assortment of audiences." After 1970, Karen's audience was, in effect, the entire world.

Plus, someone who suffers from the condition is certainly going to look different as the months and years pass by, simply because of the physical toll it takes on them.

Did not enough people at that time notice that Karen had profound issues that needed serious and immediate attention? Was she so skilled at deflecting concern, at hiding her private struggles, that many in her circle were fooled into thinking that there was no imminent problem, and certainly not one of such critical magnitude?

How is it that someone who had a career of just a dozen active years—a career that in many ways she seemed at times to regret—is still so beloved, and still fascinates so many people, more than three decades after her death?

These are some of the themes I explore in this book, which, it is important to point out, is not a biography. It was not my goal to rediscover, revisit, and rebuild as many individual details and anecdotes as possible. Nor did I wish to locate all the people who walked into and out of Karen's life, to reconstruct the dates on which everything occurred, or to re-document and then reexamine all the finer points of sales statistics and chart positions. Others have previously gone that grueling biographical route, to great achievement, most recently Randy Schmidt with *Little Girl Blue: The Life of Karen Carpenter* from 2010. I was far more interested in giving fans, who already know most of the biographical details, a little additional food for thought, a chance to further contemplate what was, why it was, and what could have been. I also wanted to prove—for those who stubbornly refuse to believe it and would never bother to wonder why—that the Carpenters are still enormously popular today, particularly Karen.

Certainly a life *is* made up of stories and anecdotes, and I do share many of those, as well, but only as a way of trying to get to know Karen a little better, or if we cannot do that, then to better appreciate what she accomplished and left behind.

There can be no decisive answers, only questions, conjectures, deductions, and opinions. For even if Richard Carpenter one day decides to be entirely forthcoming with everything he knew, sensed, assumed, or even just wondered about Karen, we still would not get a full, accurate, or inclusive portrait, simply because he wasn't inside his sister's head. Despite the Pepsodent Twins image, with which they struggled and grew to dislike immensely, they were two completely differently people—albeit inexorably allied—and for Karen's part alone, she was enormously complex.

Their alliance, incidentally, is why there can be no discussion of Karen's life and career without a significant amount of space being devoted to Richard's. Because in more ways than one, there would have been no Karen without Richard.

It matters little if I am as successful as I hope to be in leading readers through a rewarding exploration or assessment into Karen's many lives. Because anyone, at any time, and these days in almost any place, can find a way to listen to and enjoy all the music that Karen and Richard made in their glory days.

What's more, you don't even have to worry about getting slammed against a locker these days. At least I hope you don't.

1.
Innocence and Melancholia

"Walkin' around, some kind of lonely clown."

from "Rainy Days and Mondays," on the album, Carpenters.

Lonely? Karen Carpenter? A woman whose voice attracted hundreds of thousands of people to sold-out concerts in the Americas, Europe, Asia, and beyond? A singer who helped sell more than 100 million records, made more than sixty appearances on television, and for years was prominently featured in newspaper and magazine stories around the globe? A pop icon who received many love letters and marriage proposals, and who dated famous men like Mark Harmon, Tony Danza, and Steve Martin?

How can a woman like that be lonely?

It must be considered a rhetorical question, for most everyone knows that talent and celebrity immunes no one from the complexities of inner demons, unfulfilled emotional needs, and many other problems that can plague the best, brightest, and most gifted among us. Such complexities turn celebrities into enigmas and cut the stories of their lives into pieces of large, incomplete puzzles.

If not for the fact that people around the world are still talking about Karen and listening to her music—thirty-three years after she succumbed to heart failure at the age of thirty-two, brought on by her own self-destructive behavior—we might have little interest in trying to solve the puzzle of her own life. Yet people *are* still talking about her. In fact, in some ways she gets more press now, at least digitally, than she did during the Carpenters' prime in the 1970s. For all the records the group sold back then, the number of times Internet surfers and digital consumers listen to Carpenters songs today may exceed even that.

Karen, who had her first studio contract at age sixteen, recorded and performed for half her thirty-two years, and was a superstar for almost as long. During her lifetime, the Carpenters released eleven albums and thirty singles, embarked on several tours in the U.S., England, Australia, Belgium, the Netherlands, and Japan, and became fabulously rich. Their hits instantly bring baby boomers back to the era, with memories of little AM radios crackling out "(They Long to Be) Close to You," "We've Only Just Begun," "For All We Know," "Rainy Days and Mondays," "Superstar," "Hurting Each Other," "It's Going to Take Some Time This Time," "Goodbye to Love," and "I Won't Last a Day Without You."

And those nine hit records came out in just the first two-and-a-half years of the Carpenters' heyday!

Karen's resonant contralto singing voice, which actually spanned more than three octaves, was widely regarded as pure, flawless, and poignant. As young as she was, when singing, Karen had the capacity to mine complex emotions the way older singers with more life experience are able to do; it probably helped that so many of the songs were about anguish and longing, about craving the past and fearing the future, all of which, to some degree, were part of her own inner life. She had virtually no formal vocal training, but demonstrated an innate ability to slant notes, delay syllables, or use other deceptively simple techniques to achieve a desired effect. That was as much flair as she allowed. Mostly, she sang the melody as written, with just enough flourish to put her own stamp on it. She never performed acrobatics around a note the way many pop singers do today, and have been doing for the last twenty-five years in a misguided effort to prove vocal talent. She didn't have to. *Rolling Stone* writer and critic Tom Nolan called her singing voice "chilling perfection with much warmth," said that it personified "youth with wisdom," and noted that "she seems to be someone who knows something of life."

Some of the music industry's most respected luminaries have heaped on Karen's gift praise that is nothing short of astonishing. Elton John called hers "one of the greatest voices of our lifetime." Paul McCartney said she had "the best female voice in the world: melodic, tuneful and distinctive." Henry Mancini commented that "Karen had a quality about her that was so vulnerable, so exposed, that she just demanded attention. Whatever she sang came right from the heart."

Robert Hilburn, at one time a pop music critic for the *Los Angeles Times*, and one of the critics who didn't even like Carpenters too much, said that he was attracted to the "intimacy and warmth of Karen's singing—a strange but seductive blend of innocence and melancholia." In a similar vein, Dee Snider, singer and songwriter for the heavy metal band Twisted Sister, once addressed the fact that many people who would never admit they listened to the Carpenters would secretly do so whenever the opportunity arose. "When you were alone in the car by yourself and one of those catchy Carpenter tunes came on, you'd find your singing along," Snider said on the VH1 network's *I Love the 70s* special from 2003. Even before the Carpenters were famous, Karen was lauded by many who would soon be colleagues. In 1969, shortly after signing with A&M Records, she and Richard provided cabaret entertainment at several movie premiers, including an event for the new Peter O'Toole and Petula Clark film, *Goodbye, Mr. Chips*, which had music and lyrics by Leslie Bricusse. Both Bricusse and Clark (who would later become a friend of Karen's) were overheard enthusing about the pleasing and unique quality of Karen's singing voice.

Still, for every couple of fans there are a few who claim a true disdain for Richard and Karen and what they represented musically. Some regard Karen's voice as dull and impassive. Sprinkled sporadically within the thousands of pages of online comments are some that refer to the Carpenters' music, powered by Karen's voice, as "sticky sweet," "pop nonsense," and similar expressions of scorn.

In 2008, in one of its popular and prominent polls, *Rolling Stone* rated Karen almost at the bottom of their list of the top 100 greatest singers of all time, #94. While preparing an episode of *All Things Considered* on National Public Radio, during which Karen and the Rolling Stone rating were to be discussed, producer Graham Smith said that just getting on the list at all, regardless of position, is a mark of indisputable talent. That may be true, but at the same time it is an abhorrent notion to devoted fans that ninety-three other singers came ahead of Karen, including Neil Young (#37) and Bob Dylan (#7).

Karen rated a much better position on VH1's *100 Greatest Women of Rock and Roll* show, broadcast in 1999 (and selected by a panel of women). She came in at #29, just in front of Barbra Streisand and Rickie Lee Jones, and behind Carly Simon and Joan Baez.

It really isn't ratings, surveys, or even chart numbers, however, that speak to Karen's true command. For that we really need to look no farther than what she did in the recording studio. That's where she was in her true element, where she thrived, and where she felt the most vital and alive. In many ways, the studio was the safest and sanest place for her. Record buyers loved hearing her voice on LPs and singles, and fans who heard her sing in concert enjoyed the experience very much. But those who had the chance to personally observe her working in a recording studio felt the most indulged. Following her death, only a few people were able to hear the master tapes of her unembellished voice (although some tapes have found their way onto YouTube), and those are the recordings that reveal her most enduring appeal.

Al Schmitt, a multiple Grammy Award-winning recording engineer and producer who has worked with Steely Dan, Natalie Cole, Jefferson Airplane, Paul McCartney, and dozens of other top performers, had to struggle to find the words he was looking for when discussing the pleasure he felt hearing those playbacks.

"Listening to her voice and the pitch and how she could hold a note, it was absolutely remarkable," Schmitt said on an interview show called *The Download*, originating at 91.7 FM in Palm Springs, CA. "It was just amazing. My assistant and I would look at one another and say, Oh my God, can you believe this?" It was, at times, hard to believe.

Syndicated disc jockey and radio host Charlie Tuna, who interviewed Karen many times, recalls how she often told him just how much she loved making music in a recording studio. "Karen," he says, "knew she was born to sing."

2.
Teeny Grandmas and Burly Bikers

Carpenters Forever

-The title of a 2010 Japanese album by Karen Carpenter sound-alike Keiko Toge

Karen's gone, yet her legacy is not just alive and well, but growing around the world. Even after all these years, and with the true face of her darkest struggles still largely unknown, she still fascinates.

Over the last several years, from coast to coast and continent to continent, there have been tributes and media retrospectives both about the Carpenters as a group and about Karen herself. Her online presence today rivals that of many *current* groups and entertainers. Bands presently touring in the U.S. and abroad have names such as We've Only Just Begun and Carpenters Magic. Efforts have been underway for several years to have the Carpenters named to the Rock 'n Roll Hall of Fame and to have a Broadway musical created and produced based on Karen's life and career. There have been books, plays, songs, and documentaries since the 1980s in which Karen has been either the central character or a decisively important element. Carpenter memorabilia, from shirts and mugs to ticket stubs and key rings, are sold for top prices; a Carpenters poster signed by Richard and Karen recently was advertised online for $2,900, and a copy of the 1965 Downey High School yearbook sells for $250—all the more remarkable since Karen graduated in 1967. There are also at least two Carpenters-related tours in Southern California.

Rick Henry, a fan at the forefront of the Broadway musical effort, also runs several of the Karen Carpenter websites and one of the most popular Karen Carpenter Facebook pages. "I'm not sure how the Broadway effort actually began, but one of my regular Facebook readers brought it to my attention," says Henry, who subsequently began posting news about the Broadway venture on his various social media platforms. He also sent e-mails to his network of over 3,000 readers. It was all part of an attempt to try to get as many people as possible to add Karen's name to an independent poll that has been circulating online asking them what topics they'd like to see turned into stage musicals. "We did it," Henry proudly reports. "We got out the vote and put Karen at the top of that poll!"

No one can predict whether or not that will actually happen on Broadway, although in 2014 the Popejoy theatre center at the University of New Mexico presented a new show called *Yesterday Once More*, with several Carpenters songs and dramatized anecdotes about the cultural scene throughout the 1970s.

Henry's LeadSister website, in addition to providing information and video links about the group, also markets dozens of items such as Karen Carpenter t-shirts, Carpenters logo decals, and even little tin boxes with reproductions of the *Rolling Stone* cover photo shot by Annie Leibovitz, which features Karen with a goofy expression partially hidden by a red wide-brimmed hat.

A passionate fan in Champaign, IL has been holding Karen Carpenter memorial events in his home for years. Two entrepreneurs in Southern California lead tours of places in and around the town of Downey, CA, where Karen and Richard lived, worked, and owned property. One such tour is a four- to five-hour excursion to the Carpenter family home, some of Karen's favorite restaurants, and many other locations. A portion of the tour proceeds is donated in Karen's name to the National Eating Disorders Association.

The Carpenter home in Downey has been in the news recently because of the current owner's plan to raze it, much to the chagrin of thousands of outraged fans. According to newspaper reports, the owner was tired of all the people who visited asking to be let inside.

There have been almost a dozen televised documentaries over the years, including *Living Famously: Karen Carpenter*, *Only Yesterday: the Carpenters' Story*, *Close to You: Remembering the Carpenters*, and *Autopsy: The Last Hours of Karen Carpenter*. The syndicated American television show *A Current Affair* devoted an entire episode to the singer, which they titled "The Karen Carpenter Cover-Up." In addition to Ray Coleman's 1994 biography called *The Carpenters: The Untold Story*, written with Richard's cooperation, and Randy Schmidt's biography, *Little Girl Blue*, there are also several self-published books in which Karen's anorexia and early death are examined, or in which she is reincarnated with the author placing her into his own savior fantasy.

In 1987, independent filmmaker Todd Haynes directed a short film called *Superstar: The Karen Carpenter Story*, using Barbie dolls to illustrate the singer's rise and fall—with a no-holds-barred narrative—along with Carpenters' songs on the soundtrack that Haynes used without proper licensing. Richard successfully sued Haynes to withdraw the film from circulation, although it has evolved into a cult favorite since then. Haynes was a college student at the time he made the film on a shoestring budget, but he did move into the professional ranks afterward with such directorial work as 2007's *I'm Not There* about Bob Dylan, which featured Richard Gere and Cate Blanchett (Haynes had Dylan's permission), and the 2011 HBO miniseries *Mildred Pierce*, starring Kate Winslet.

A 1995 album called *If I Were a Carpenter* featured some of the group's songs performed by Sonic Youth, Sheryl Crow, the Cranberries and others. It sold extremely well. In 2005, Olivia Newton-John, one of Karen's dearest friends, recorded an album called *Indigo: Women of Song*, honoring several artists, and on it was her tribute version of "Rainy Days and Mondays."

Based on the promotional plugs that can be found online, claiming to sound like Karen is deemed to carry a marketing advantage. Dozens of independently produced CDs sold on digital sites such as CDBaby and Amazon eagerly play up the angle with such tags as "Evoking the sound of Karen Carpenter," "Echoes of Karen Carpenter," and "With the warmth of Karen Carpenter."

There is even a song called "Downey Girl" by Dave Alvin, a singer, songwriter, guitarist, and record producer, who has been with such bands as the Blasters, X, and the Knitters. Alvin, who *Rolling Stone* called "an under-recognized guitar hero," admits through his "Downey Girl" lyrics that he was never a Carpenters fan, but was undeniably touched by her untimely passing: "And then I hear her singing on the car radio, a sweet suburban song from a long time ago, and I think about her sadness, and I think about her pain, and for four sweet minutes I'm back home again. 'Cause she was a Downey Girl." Alvin also grew up in Downey.

In 2012, a satirical musical comedy played in Los Angeles entitled *Are You There, God? It's Me, Karen Carpenter*. It was inspired by a Judy Blume children's book.

For as many musical luminaries who had shared their affection for Karen's talent when she was still alive, there have been an equal number in the days since. Madonna's 1993 single, "Rain," from her *Erotica* album, was a tribute to Karen, whom she held in high esteem. "Karen Carpenter had the clearest, purest voice," she wrote in publicity material for the album. "I'm completely influenced by her harmonic sensibility." Similarly, Gwen Stefani's comment about Karen's voice has been cited in the media a number of times: "It doesn't matter how many times you hear it; you'll still get goose bumps when you hear her sing."

Doug Haverty, who was the director of international publicity and marketing at the Carpenters' record label from 1977 to 1991, is just one of many industry veterans who confirm the enduring fascination with Karen and with the Carpenters. "I can't tell you how many times people from all walks of life and all around the world have confessed to me, when they find out that I worked at A&M, how much they appreciate the music of the Carpenters. And that includes singers and composers who have been inspired by them. And then, when they discover I actually worked with Richard and Karen, the confessions simple cascade."

There are many tribute groups currently on tour, with young ladies set upon duplicating Karen's translucent voice. A West Coast-based show called *Close to You* features Michelle Whited, who has been asked to sing many times for the U.S. Air Force Orchestra and has sung at pre-game shows for the Seattle Seahawks, the Seattle SuperSonics, the Los Angeles Lakers, and other professional sports teams. A program in Florida called *The Carpenters Tribute Show* uses a full band and spotlights a Chicago-bred vocalist named Pam Zeitler, who has also lent her talents to bands that pay tribute to the Manhattan Transfer and the Mamas and the Papas. A band out of England called Carpenters Magic features cabaret singer Jenny Sinclair, who, in addition to touring extensively and playing many different kinds of venues, has also released two tribute albums, *Forever Carpenters* and *One More Time*. ("One More Time" is the name of a Carpenters song from their 1976 album, *A Kind of Hush*.)

A Canadian singer named Roxanne Charette performs a Karen Carpenter tribute called *Yesterday Once More*, and has taken the show to several countries. Now based in Nashville, she has won top honors from Canada's country music industry. In Australia, singer Julie Bridge does her own *Karen Carpenter Tribute* across the nation. In Japan, where the Carpenters have been exceedingly popular for years, Keiko Toge, whose singing voice bears a strong resemblance to Karen's, has appeared in concert—at least once with an appreciative Richard in attendance—and has recorded several Carpenters tunes. One of her more recent albums, entirely devoted to the group, is titled *Carpenters Forever*.

"Sheena Easton told me what a big fan of Karen's she is," notes Michelle Berting Brett, the lead singer of the tribute band, We've

Only Just Begun, which tours the country playing big casinos as well as smaller nightclubs. "David Sanborn, the jazz saxophonist, is a huge fan, too. He broke out into 'Superstar' when we were talking to each other about Karen." Brett says she is pleasantly surprised at the diversity of the people who love Carpenters music, and who especially love Karen's voice. "Fans I've met include teeny grandmas and burly bikers. It's actually quite enjoyable to see. It seems as if a lot of people just seek the comfort of simple music sung in a sweetly passionate way. That's all they want. And that's what Karen gave."

3.
The Impact and the Crush

"Hey guys, this is gonna last a lot longer than three years!"

–Doug Strawn, longtime instrumentalist with the Carpenters

It took someone outside the immediate family to categorically assert, perhaps for the first time, that Karen should sing instead of settling to be a tagalong sister who played the drums. That's not to say that Richard, and Agnes and Harold Carpenter, their parents, did not recognize that Karen had an unambiguous vocal talent; they did, but it doesn't seem as if they pinpointed it as something exceptionally unique that would one day lead to fame and fortune.

Karen started exhibiting the qualities that made her voice distinctive when she was in high school, yet even with that knowledge, she may have been too self-conscious, and perhaps not even driven or industrious enough, to have carved out a career in music on her own without Richard by her side. He was the one who took the lead in forming bands and pursuing record contracts. Without him, Karen's singular and instantly recognizable singing voice might have gone forever unrecognized. After all, as they were growing up, while Richard practiced the piano and poured over sheet music inside the house, Karen much preferred to stay outside playing softball.

Richard Lynn Carpenter was born October 15, 1946, in New Haven, CT. He took to piano, music theory, and composition quickly and easily, and played records incessantly all through his childhood. Among his favorites were Les Paul and Mary Ford, Spike Jones, and Teresa Brewer, whose 1949 record, "Music! Music! Music! (Put Another Nickel In)," provided the title for a Carpenters TV special more than three decades later. That special, *The Carpenters: Music, Music, Music*, aired in 1980. For a time, beginning when he was sixteen, Richard studied piano at Yale University's School of Music.

Karen Anne arrived March 2, 1950. Her love of outdoor play notwithstanding, when she was little she did often sit with her brother to listen to those records. She tried, for a short time, to learn the flute in elementary school. As most children do, she mulled over several professions in her head when thinking about what she might like to do as a grownup. Three that came up quite often were commercial artist, nurse, and airline stewardess. She later chuckled over the last two, not caring for the sight of blood and spending more time in airplanes than she ever wanted to remember.

In 1963, Harold and Agnes moved the family to Downey, CA, a suburb of Los Angeles, to improve Richard's chances of eventually building a career as an arranger and composer. (Also, they didn't like the harsh New England winters.) Richard enrolled at California State University, Long Beach, to study music. Karen attended Downey High School where, after an aborted attempt to master the glockenspiel, she took up a completely different kind of percussion instrument. She saw a talented friend of hers named Frankie Chavez playing drums, and became captivated by their complexity and versatility. Certainly, the instrument's significance in establishing rhythm did not escape her, either. She decided to give 'the skins' a try.

"Everybody kind of looked at me funny, but I really didn't care," she told TV interviewer Jerry Dunphy in 1972 when he asked her about taking up the drums.

Karen proved to have an amazing facility for percussion almost immediately. (Barely a decade later, readers of *Playboy* magazine named Karen "Best Drummer of the Year" in its 1975 music poll.) At home, before her parents decided to buy her a set of her own,

Karen was known to drum on whatever surfaces were available, such as bar stools, using anything she could get her hands on to bang them with, like chopsticks.

In 1965, Richard and Karen, along with Wes Jacobs, a friend of Richard's from Cal State who played the upright bass and the tuba, formed a jazz combo called the Richard Carpenter Trio. Karen wasn't interested in singing for the trio, so a young woman named Margaret Shanor took on that role and stayed on as their vocalist for a while. In the spring of the following year, Joe Osborn, one of the top studio musicians on the West Coast and a partner in a small label called Magic Lamp Records, heard Karen sing when she and Richard were providing accompaniment for another friend in Osborn's garage studio. Years later, Osborn said in a television documentary that he was the one who recommended they concentrate on Karen's vocals as the key to an eventual recording career. *Wow! What about her?* he recalled thinking, realizing how well she sung.

Richard, interviewed for the same documentary, said he agreed, admitting that once he heard his sister's singing voice carried from a high-quality microphone to a professional monitor—which hadn't always been the case at home—he was sold on the idea that Karen's voice was indeed very special.

Karen, at sixteen, was signed to Magic Lamp as a vocalist. Richard was signed a few days later as a songwriter with the company's publishing arm, Light-Up Music. Unfortunately, Magic Lamp had little money for promotion and folded the following year.

During the time that they were hoping for some industry recognition through their Magic Lamp association, the Richard Carpenter Trio played in the "Battle of the Bands" at the Hollywood Bowl and won Best Combo and a separate trophy for acquiring the highest score of all the competing bands. Richard also won for Outstanding Instrumentalist. About the "Battle of the Bands" competition, Leonard Feather wrote in the *Los Angeles Times*, "The musical surprise of the evening was the trio of Richard Carpenter, a remarkably original soloist . . . Flanking his piano were Karen Carpenter, his talented sixteen year old sister, at the drums, and bassist Wes Jacobs, who doubled amusingly and confidently on tuba."

After that show—the same day, in fact—Richard was approached by Neely Plumb, a preeminent artist-and-repertoire executive with RCA-Victor Records, who asked if the trio would be interested in cutting some test tracks for the label. Plumb, in addition to other roles in the industry, was also a noted arranger, conductor, instrumentalist, and soundtrack producer. At first, Richard declined, smugly telling Plumb that they already had a record contract—although what Richard was referring to was the solo contract Karen had with Magic Lamp and his own contract as a songwriter. Those contracts, of course, had little to do with the music Plumb had heard at the Hollywood Bowl from the award-winning trio.

When Richard reassessed the offer, he retracted his refusal and a deal was reached. Richard, Karen, and Wes cut eleven tracks at RCA, but as fate would have it at the time, RCA's studio executives were unconvinced that the work the three young musicians recorded had any commercial viability and decided not to continue the relationship. The Richard Carpenter Trio no longer had a label.

In 1967, Jacobs departed, and Richard formed a group that first he called the Summerchimes, and then Spectrum. Spectrum (which included a female vocalist named Leslie Johnson, who Karen befriended after she enrolled that fall at California State, Long Beach) recorded several demos to send to record companies and also tried to make a name for themselves by playing at The Whiskey a Go-Go, The Troubadour, Ledbetter's, and other popular nightclubs around Los Angeles. They had various levels of success. Sometimes the crowds danced, which the club owners and managers took as a validation that hiring the neophyte group in the first place was a wise move; other times the crowd felt compelled to listen to the innovative sounds Spectrum was playing *instead* of dancing which, ironically and lamentably, the owners and managers took as a bad sign.

While success on the club circuit was an ebb and flow affair, it flowed enough to compel two record companies to dangle recording contracts in front of Spectrum's collective eyes. The first was Uni, which was no small operation; the company's name was short for Universal City Records and was owned by the media giant MCA. (Neil Diamond signed with the label in 1968.) The second, White Whale, had less of a corporate pedigree than Uni, but a solid return thanks to their #1 protégé, the Turtles. Richard, however, was not entirely pleased with the contract terms offered by either firm. First he turned down White Whale, and then he found out that Uni turned *him* down because of the amount of time that had passed since the initial offer.

Spectrum, still without a label, disbanded, but Richard had by then decided that he and Karen could get along on their own. Karen still considered herself primarily a drummer, but Richard knew that her voice held certain qualities that could make them stand apart; he also sensed that it could be the foundation of true marketable strength and individuality, especially if he continued to build on the vocal overdubbing techniques he was beginning to master, techniques that created rich harmonies using just Karen's distinctive voice, along with his own. That, in fact, was a style he had first admired when he was a boy in New Haven listening to records and radio broadcasts featuring the multi-tracked harmonies of Les Paul and Mary Ford.

Still attending Cal State Long Beach, Richard had by this time received a student deferment, thereby avoiding the Vietnam draft, and moved forward on his musical plans for a brand new group, without fear of interruption. Richard wanted to call the new group Carpenters (not *the* Carpenters), which, in addition to him and his sister, also included Bill Sissyoev on bass. (It may have been their official name, but it never stuck with the public or the press.) In June 1968, the Carpenters appeared on *Your*

All-American College Show on television, and Richard once again began submitting demo tapes to every record label in Hollywood.

It is not uncommon in the music business for a chain of fortuitous connections to help foster the right-place/right-time scenario that sometimes leads to success. Such was the case with Richard and Karen.

An old friend of Richard's, Ed Sulzer, who had earlier lent Richard a hand by circulating demo tapes around Southern California, had just come back into the picture. Sulzer, in turn, had another friend named Jack Daugherty, who he thought could help the effort to pass demos along because of Daugherty's connections in the music business. Daugherty, who had been a trumpet player in the Woody Herman band, retired from music in the early 1960s to work in corporate public relations, but maintained ties with several people in the industry, including a member of Herb Alpert's Tijuana Brass. Alpert was one of the principals at A&M Records. Sure enough, Dougherty did eventually manage to get a Carpenters demo tape into Alpert's hands.

Herb Alpert—the A in A&M—approached the record business somewhat differently from many of his colleagues at other labels. He had founded the company in 1962 with his business partner, Jerry Moss—the M in the corporate name. Alpert believed as much in the discovery and nurturing of talent as he did in the financial independence that came along with hits. By signing the Carpenters, he wasn't necessarily hoping to tap into current trends or to replicate a style that had already proven itself commercially lucrative; instead, he was looking for groups and individuals with musical passion that could eventually translate into profitability. When he initially met Richard and Karen and listened to their music, he sensed both the passion and the potential. Jerry Moss formally signed the siblings to A&M in April 1969.

"When I first heard Karen's voice I was charmed. It was love at first hear," Alpert said in the PBS documentary, *Close to You: Remembering the Carpenters*. He was referring to the demo tape he had agreed to listen to.

More recently he said, "When I heard Karen and Richard's tape, I closed my eyes, sitting on my couch at A&M in my office, and her voice sounded like she was sitting right next to me."

The week following their official admission into the A&M family of recording artists, Richard and Karen began work on an album called *Offering*, which was released in October. It sold just 18,000 copies and lost money for A&M, but Alpert was known to support his artists and give them room to grow, so he kept them on. The sole single that was released from the album was a ballad version of Lennon and McCartney's "Ticket to Ride" that showcased Karen's vocal range—she spans three octaves in the song—and also highlighted the multilayered, chorus-like arrangements on which Richard excelled. The single reached #54 on the *Billboard* chart, and while not a member of the exclusive Top 40 club, #54 wasn't far off, either. The song is hardly ever associated with the Carpenters' rise to fame, but in a way it did support Alpert's hunch that there was something special that deserved a nurturing chance. (When *Offering* was re-released after the Carpenters' first hit, the name of the album was changed to *Ticket to Ride*.)

The summer of 1970, like many summers before and after, welcomed a broad assortment of events and diversions, on the air, on screen, on TV, and on the national stage. The Beatles' *Let It Be* album reached the top of the charts, as did their "Long and Winding Road" single, which shared Top 40 radio time with such diverse fare as "Teach Your Children" by Crosby, Still, Nash & Young, "Which Way You Goin', Billy?" by the Poppy Family, "Band of Gold" by Freda Payne, and "The Wonder of You" by Elvis Presley. Brand new in the movie theatres were the anti-war satire *Catch-22*, a Disney flick called *The Boatnicks*, the musical *On a Clear Day You Can See Forever*, and another war film, the action-comedy *Kelly's Heroes*. Most TV shows were on hiatus, but viewers eagerly awaited the fall return of *Rowan and Martin's Laugh-In*, *Mannix*, *Marcus Welby, M.D.*, *The Brady Bunch*, and the final season of *The Ed Sullivan Show*. On May 4, Ohio National Guardsmen opened fire at Kent State University during an anti-war protest, killing four students and wounding nine others. Also that month, while the Soviets tested nuclear bombs at least four times within U.S.S.R. borders, the United States tested one in the state of Nevada. There were race riots in Georgia, Jim Bouton was criticized by the baseball commissioner for writing a book called *Ball Four*, and President Nixon signed the 26th Amendment that lowered the national voting age to eighteen.

Into this mix came a song about angels getting together and deciding to create a dream come true. It was called "(They Long to Be) Close to You."

Earlier in the year, Herb Alpert had given Richard the lead sheet of that song to consider recording. It was a seven-year-old composition by Burt Bacharach and Hal David that was first released as a single by actor Richard Chamberlain in 1963, appeared on a 1964 Dionne Warwick album, and was then slated to be Alpert's follow-up to his 1968 hit, "This Guy's In Love With You." But Alpert ultimately decided that he wasn't interested, and gave it to Richard instead. Richard wrote a new arrangement (he actually arranged several versions, per Alpert's request), and the Carpenters recorded it. It debuted on coast to coast radio at the end of June 1970 and rose through the rankings to reach the top spot on July 25.

The next single, released about a month later, was "We've Only Just Begun," written by Paul Williams and Roger Nichols, which Richard had first heard, in a shorter version, on television when it was the theme song for a bank commercial. It reached #2. The single after that, "For All We Know," reached #3. Richard became aware of "For All We Know" when he went to see the movie *Lovers and Other Strangers*. Written by Fred Karlin, Robb Royer, and Jimmy Griffin (Royer and Griffin were founding members of the group Bread), the song accompanies a wedding scene in the movie; once the Carpenters' version was released, it blossomed into a popular wedding song, along with "We've Only Just Begun," and remained that way for more than a generation.

Although still relative novices in the national spotlight, in October, Richard and Karen strode onto one of the most popular and daunting stages in television history, *The Ed Sullivan Show*. They had already appeared on national network TV, on *The Dating Game*, *The Tonight Show*, and *The David Frost Show*, but *The Ed Sullivan Show* was, arguably, the most impressive of the lot: it was live, had a long, storied history, and was watched religiously by more than 12 million viewers every Sunday night. If that wasn't daunting enough, appearing on the same evening as the Carpenters were legendary performers B.B. King, Tony Bennett, and George Burns. Karen, who was just twenty years old (Richard had turned twenty-four three days before the broadcast), handled herself with grace and confidence.

There was no stopping them now. Ten months, ten television appearances, and several million dollars in sales after their first hit, they appeared at New York's famed Carnegie Hall—another venue that, like *The Ed Sullivan Show*, is frequently associated with artists who have earned their way there through hard work and more than a few hard knocks. For these young artists, Carnegie Hall was only the beginning.

It didn't take long for the Carpenters to become internationally famous, and to earn in several months what their parents could never have imagined earning in a lifetime. The record label, of course, benefited momentously from their touch, and the timing could not have been better for Herb Alpert and Jerry Moss; prior to the chart reign of the Carpenters, A&M had not had a hit since Alpert's own "This Guy's In Love With You" topped the charts in June 1968, and as a result the company had been facing a bleak financial outlook.

Despite the sudden influx of funds that A&M was now able to use for state-of-the-art equipment and aggressive marketing campaigns, it had been rumored that some of the artists in the studio family were not especially happy to be professionally associated with the Carpenters. After all, the group was quickly coming to be regarded as chaste and antiseptic—images few musical acts want hanging around them.

An A&M client mutiny was unlikely, however, for despite the overall persona of the Carpenters, the skills and influence that both Richard and Karen brought with them to the company were undeniable, and that often *is* an image with which professionals like to be associated. Before long, Richard was respected across the board as a consummate arranger, instrumentalist, and producer. (Jack Daugherty, who made the opportune connection between the demo tape and A&M, was listed as the group's producer on their first few albums.) For her part, Karen had a charming personality to go along with her incomparable voice, and everyone at the studio and in the industry adored her.

"They were a new band, and new bands hardly last any longer than three years, at best. But early on with the Carpenters, it was pretty clear that something special was going on," said long-time Carpenters' band member Doug Strawn, who played keyboards, woodwinds, and sang duets with Karen many times during their early shows. (Strawn passed away in 2013.)

"I remember we were at the Impact Tavern in Bellevue, Washington," Strawn recalled. "It was really just a dance gig. Richard told the audience that we were going to play a song that had been released only a short time before called 'We've Only Just Begun.' I played those now-famous first six notes on the clarinet, and I wasn't looking at the audience when I played it. But when I finally opened my eyes, I noticed a crush. Everyone came up close to the stage. Boys had their arms around their girlfriends. They were mesmerized by the song in general and by Karen in particular. And I remember saying to one of the guys in the band, 'Hey, you know something, this is gonna last a lot longer than three years!'"

Though it would become clearer in the months and years ahead, one of the primary reasons that Strawn's prediction became a reality was because of the complementary musical capabilities of Richard and Karen. In addition to his own formidable skill, Richard was able to avail himself of his sister's vocal flair; in addition to her own unparalleled gift, Karen benefited from the production insights and determined efforts of her brother. We might never have heard of either Carpenter had not Richard and Karen been on the ride together.

In addition to needing each other, it is also possible that Richard and Karen needed the 1970s. Most artists are, in one way or another, a product of their times, and the Carpenters, as exceptional as they may have been, were no exception. David Browne, a contributing editor at *Rolling Stone* magazine, and the author of several books on the music business, put it best when he said that the U.S. was getting exceedingly tired from the war in Vietnam, from college protests, and from many broken promises from the national stage, and that many people were simply looking for something new. "What everyone—especially rock fans verging on age thirty—wanted was quiet, and pop was there to serve," he wrote in his 2011 book *Fire and Rain: the Beatles, Simon & Garfunkel, James Taylor, CSNY and the Lost Story of 1970.* A big part of that quiet change, Browne wrote, was ". . . the Carpenters, a brother-sister duo from Southern California, who looked like student-council candidates and made polite music to match . . ." Their numerous Top 10 hits that year, Browne noted, proved that "America wanted more, please. Elsewhere on the radio that fall were Bread's 'It Don't Matter to Me,' Elton John's 'Your Song,' Gordon Lightfoot's 'If You Could Read My Mind,' and Cat Stevens' 'Wild World'—a parade of balladeers," he concluded, "with less interest in making a racket and more in expressing their innermost feelings . . . ."

But throughout the 1970s, Richard and Karen Carpenter built a catalog of music that was more than just quiet and polite, that went beyond ballads, and that were more than just expressions of our innermost feelings. In fact, the breadth of their directory of songs surprises even many fans, its range limited only by the relatively short amount of time that Karen was around to record. She and Richard were with A&M for just under fourteen years—and a lot of that time was taken up by touring, promotional activities, dealing with personal issues, and other matters. Still, the range speaks for itself. Their smoky rendition of "This Masquerade" could hardly be more different from the country-flavored "Sweet, Sweet Smile," nor the beseeching love song "I Won't Last a Day Without You" from the childlike "Rainbow Connection." One of the oldest songs the Carpenters recorded was composed for the 1935 Broadway musical, *Jumbo*, by Richard Rodgers, Lorenz Hart, and Irving Kahal. By contrast, one of the newest was written in 1981, giving the Carpenters' catalog a musical span of forty-six years. The 1981 song, "(Want You) Back in My Life Again," was a synthesizer-fused number co-written by Kerry Michael Chater, a one-time member of Gary Puckett and The Union Gap. (The synthesizer was played by Daryl Dragon of The Captain and Tennille.)

The Carpenter catalog contains plenty of up-tempo songs, moody ballads, minimally-orchestrated pop tunes, and sophisticated productions that required dozens of hired instrumentalists and countless hours behind the mixing board. There were some borrowed from the movies and the stage, some that barely predated versions by other popular artists of the day, such as Anne Murray and Barry Manilow, and many that derived their power from Karen's own emotional state of mind. John Bettis, who wrote the lyrics to dozens of Carpenters songs, with Richard as composer, knew Karen well, cared about her, and understood her melancholy mood, which he said was an emotion he often shared. "I Need to Be in Love," which he wrote with Richard (and Albert Hammond), became one of Karen's favorite Carpenters songs of all time:

"I used to say, 'No promises, let's keep it simple'
But freedom only helps you say goodbye
It took a while for me to learn that nothin' comes for free
The price I've paid is high enough for me.

I know I need to be in love
I know I've wasted too much time
I know I ask perfection from a quite imperfect world
And fool enough to think that's what I've found."

Though they recorded professionally for just slightly more than a dozen years, the musical palette of the Carpenters was quite vivid. What further distinguishes their rise is that it took only a few months from the time Jerry Moss first signed the duo for them to receive the highest recognition from their own peers. On March 16, 1971, Richard and Karen attended the 13th annual Grammy Awards as nominees for Best Contemporary Vocal Performance by a Duo, Group or Chorus. Their competition included the Jackson Five, Simon and Garfunkel, Chicago, and the Beatles. The Carpenters won. They also won the Best New Artist award.

When Shirley Jones and David Cassidy, on hiatus from the second season of their hit TV series *The Partridge Family*, announced the vocal performance winners, Richard and Karen bounded to the stage—looking both pleased and awkward—to accept the award. "We still can't believe we have a record out," Richard guilelessly told the amused and appreciative crowd in the Hollywood Palladium, and then went on to thank Jack Dougherty, Herb Alpert, and Jerry Moss.

Karen seemed very happy when she saw Richard accepting the little gold gramophone from Shirley Jones.

At least she *looked* happy.

4.
The Girl Behind the Drums

"I just never saw her on top of the world. She was very hard to figure out."

-Hal Blaine, Wrecking Crew drummer

She may never have been truly happy, and we may never truly know why. No matter how much Karen's life and inner struggles are scrutinized, there will always be too many loose ends that can never be adequately tied, and too many questions that can never be fully answered.

The list of issues is a long one. For one thing, Karen had a fractious relationship with her mother, who seemed to hold her older child on a higher pedestal and, additionally, had what many described as a chilly and obstinate personality. For another, she adored and revered her brother who, intending no harm, was a taskmaster when it came to recording and the pursuit of ever-higher rungs on the ladder of success. That, in turn, affected Karen's ability to develop a personal life and an identity of her own. And for a third, she craved love and romance, but never had much luck finding and keeping it. Whether that's due more to her career or her inner character will never be entirely clear. Probably a little of both.

After an entire adolescence of mostly tomboyish behavior, and only modest interest in fashion and cosmetics, Karen was thrust into the public limelight which, at that time, decreed that being rail thin, modishly adorned, and heavily made up was the celebrity style of choice. Model Lesley Hornby, better known as Twiggy, had come to the United States in 1967, already famous, just as Karen was starting to perform in public. The nation's press, including *Life, Newsweek,* and *The New Yorker,* devoted many lengthy stories to the Twiggy look and style, which was often called a national phenomenon. Cher, another symbol of thin and ornamental splendor, had by then become not only an extremely successful contralto singer, but also a fashion icon. Sonny and Cher had nearly a dozen Top 40 singles between 1965 and 1972, just around the time that Karen, another contralto singer, was chasing the same kind of validation.

Family issues, romance issues, and self-image and self-worth issues gave Karen psychological baggage and emotional chaos that must have been beyond arduous to deal with. Yet, nearly all of her closest companions insist that she clowned around constantly, had a penchant for silly wordplay and funny voices, showed a marvelous sense of humor, never hesitated to help a friend, and absolutely adored children. By most measures, she loved the reality that life exists. She was just terribly uncomfortable with her own. As she sang in "I Won't Last a Day Without You," a Carpenters hit single from 1974, "Day after day I must face a world of strangers where I don't belong."

Evidently, she meant it.

It is quite conceivable that Karen had deeply-rooted psychological issues from childhood and may have been giving off signals for years. In public, she was so good-natured, giddy, and dedicated to her craft and career that not enough people close to her recognized those signs as being so profound that they required immediate professional intervention.

Some, however, *did* pick up on them, though at the time the gravity of it all was not yet apparent.

Legendary drummer Hal Blaine, who eventually worked with the Carpenters many times, met sixteen-year-old Karen three years before the first Carpenters album was produced, when she and her brother were trying to establish some professional ties in the Southern California music scene. He recalls that Karen always seemed a little melancholy.

"I just never saw her on top of the world. She was very hard to figure out," says Blaine, who was a member of the Wrecking Crew session band that backed the Beach Boys, the Mamas and the Papas, and other top groups of the 1960s and 1970s. "She was a sweetheart. I even had a set of drums made for her—but I just never saw her having a big laugh."

Renowned composer and recording artist Neil Sedaka has a similar recollection. After a successful decade as a songwriter and pop star in the late 1950s and early 1960s, his career stalled, but in 1975, hot off the success of the single "Laughter in the Rain," which helped spark his comeback, Sedaka was paired with the Carpenters as their opening act for a world tour.

"She was very blasé," he recalls, reminiscing about the tour. "Like she was bored or something. Everything was too much for her. On stage, though," he adds, "she was absolutely perfect."

It was as early as 1967 that Karen began to fret about her body and seek medical advice for what she considered to be a weight problem. During her preteen and teen years, she was never thin; like her mother, Karen had wide hips. Plus, as a rough-and-tumble, softball-loving girl in New Haven, she probably thought very little about achieving and maintaining the feminine physique that she craved as she entered her late teens. While she cared more for running bases than running for fancy clothes, it must have gnawed at her to hear some people refer to her as chubby. Over time she came to believe that everything she ate would, in the body-conscious vernacular, go to her hips. It troubled her greatly.

As her body changed during adolescence, she developed what society calls—often in an admiring way—an hourglass figure. She was probably not biologically predisposed to anything else, but frowned on that kind of look. When she was seventeen, a doctor recommended the Stillman diet, which required many vitamins, eight glasses of water each day, and the complete elimination of fatty foods.

Karen never denied that she preferred to play the drums instead of being out front singing. Over the years, many people, both from inside her personal and professional circles, and those who simply observed from a journalistic point of view, have suggested that her preference was attributable not just to her love of the instrument and her amazing facility for it, but also to the fact that it gave her something to hide behind. Until compelled to take center stage as the singing star that audiences bought tickets to see, she blissfully stayed behind the snare, bass, hi-hats, and tom-toms. (At five-foot-four, she could hardly be seen from her drum stool.) It was her comfort zone in more ways than one. In some of the earliest concert footage available in which she *was* out front singing, she is noticeably wider in the hips than later on—but never fat. The fact that her wardrobe in the early professional period was not as complimentary for her figure as it could have been may have intensified her discontent with the way she looked.

There is an often repeated story that her compulsion to lose weight gained momentum after reading a concert review in which the word chubby was actually used. (Just as often that story is refuted as a rumor that has merely become truth via the route of urban legend.) Whether true or not, some people whose paths she crossed on her way up used one variation or another of the word in recounting their earliest memories of meeting and working with the Carpenter siblings. (Richard, too, had been called chubby in the early days by some professional acquaintances.) The possibility exists that Karen overheard some of the comments, and if that had happened, she clearly did not have proper emotional tools to adequately deal with it.

By the time she was twenty, Karen started to have cameras pointed in her direction all the time and writers scribbling notes about her appearance whenever she showed up in public. Cameras can be unforgiving and, on occasion, so can critics, to the point where even people *with* the proper tools can sometimes forget how to use them.

The way she felt and the indelicate spoken or written words she may have heard were not the only burdens Karen carried around with her. As many have speculated, from armchair psychoanalysts to real ones, she seemed unable to stop her mother from undermining her feelings of self-worth, and powerless to stop others from controlling her career. In addition to everything else, she may have decided to control something she thought she *could* control: the way she looked.

Several people who were part of the touring entourage have stated in various published accounts that as early as 1970 Karen never ate anything resembling a real meal, and that by the mid 1970s she was dieting obsessively. It was in 1975, when her weight dropped to 91 pounds, that Karen had to take two months off from all career activities to recuperate from fatigue and a weakened physical condition.

At one point, she embarked on a rigorous exercise program, as opposed to strictly a dieting program, and was said to have developed muscles that to her represented nothing more than unsightly bulk. As many anorexics do, in time she became expert at hiding her behavior. She knew just how to push food around on her plate to make it seem as if she were eating well. She had enough skill as a natural actress to know how to make people believe she was telling the truth whenever she denied having a problem—a remarkable feat considering that she would often spend inordinate amounts of time in the bathroom, even during restaurant outings.

During those times when she was abusing laxatives (to purge herself) and thyroid medication (to speed up her metabolism), she grew confident in her ability to hide the medications so that no one would find them (although sometimes they *were* found).

Hers was an internal battle she was determined to fight alone, ill-prepared though she was to do so. It made her feel very isolated, separated from the rest of the world, exceedingly downcast. The young woman, who with friends was a clownish jester, became a 'lonely clown' when dealing with her demons, not unlike the character she sings about in the first person in the song "Rainy Days and Mondays," a hit from 1971.

It wasn't until January 1982, when Karen was thirty-one, that she went into therapy for the disorder known as anorexia nervosa. Her therapist was a specialist in New York named Steven Levenkron. The TV newsmagazine, *A Current Affair*, ran a two-part segment called "The Karen Carpenter Cover-Up" nearly a decade later in which Levenkron insisted that Karen's anorexia had been defeated by the time she left his care, and that what killed her was the enormous quantity of laxatives she took afterward. That merely raises the question that if she took an enormous quantity of laxatives afterward, was her anorexia truly defeated?

If, as Randy Schmidt reported in his biography, Karen read Levenkron's 1978 novel, *The Best Little Girl in the World*, about an anorexic girl named Kessa, clues can be detected as to why she agreed to go into therapy with the book's author. In the story, Kessa has various family experiences and makes some comments about herself that may have resonated deeply with Karen, such as the fact that Kessa's siblings, Gregg and Susanna, seemed to elicit more fondness from her mother and her father (whose name was Harold, as was Karen's), and that once Kessa is in the therapeutic care of the fictional Dr. Sherman (who readers can easily presume is really Levenkron in disguise), she feels a nurturing and caring that she gets from no one else.

"I asked for nothing, and that's what I got," Kessa cries to her father. "Gregg got admiration and Susanna got attention and I got nothing. Nothing from you and nothing from Mommy. She doesn't even like me." Elsewhere Kessa utters such remarks as "I really don't belong. Everyone else belonged, but not me," and about Dr. Sherman she says, "He doesn't make me do anything. He was so understanding."

If Karen had read the novel cover to cover, she selectively ignored the possibility that she might one day have to go through some of what Kessa has to go through in the hospital in order to return to a healthy weight—particularly the preparation for Kessa's catheter insertion. As the narrator explains, "The first sting came up high in the center of her chest. Kessa fought to keep back the tears. The fourth, below her arm, was the worst of all. The last injection seemed to go on forever, and then she felt the pain surging up her back into her neck."

On one hand, the real Karen must have identified with the fictional Kessa, but on the other, she apparently was convinced that Kessa's problems were far worse than her own.

Levenkron wrote his novel before getting to know Karen, but more than twenty years later, after treating many other anorexics, he penned the nonfiction *Anatomy of Anorexia*, in which he provides several decisive clues to the condition. Many probably reflect Karen's own psyche. Among his statements are that the typical anorexic "is a perfectionist, and the goal of losing weight becomes an all-consuming effort" that results in what he calls super-dieting, and that "the thinner the anorexic gets, the fatter she feels," having "crossed the border into psychopathology, or mental illness." Also, "Often girls who develop anorexia have a history of being nice, protective, compliant, agreeable, avoiding conflict . . . The third stage [out of five that Levenkron discusses] develops when the girl with anorexia has been criticized for becoming too thin by many around her. She has disregarded their advice, and now their demands to stop losing weight and to start gaining are renewed. At some point she realizes that for the first time in her life she has become defiant to everyone around her. She is no longer afraid of conflict."

Levenkron states elsewhere that "The most commonly known biological change that takes place on the female body during starvation is the shutdown of the reproduction system." Had she known that was a possibility, Karen, who almost more than anything else wanted to have children, may have found another way to address and defeat her personal conflicts. Serious literature on her specific condition was still relatively scarce during her lifetime, and more to the point, she probably didn't deem herself to be doing anything terribly damaging in the first place.

"I find that most anorexics are not grounded in the reality of its physical damage," says specialist Emily Rosenthal. "There's denial and there's apathy, but there's no processing of the impact of their relentless starving, binging, purging, and other dangerous behaviors."

"Anorexia is but a symptom of much deeper conflicts and issues," adds Dr. Amy Nulsen, Ph.D., who has many years of experience treating people with the condition, and who suffered from it herself as a youngster. "Among those issues are ambivalence about growing up, sexuality, separation and individuation, control, worthiness, and the inability to identify or express feelings."

Like many, Dr. Nulsen recalls that the first time she remembers hearing about anorexia in the media was when Karen passed away. Her own affliction occurred in the same general era; she partially attributes her plunge into the condition to the Twiggy effect. Dr. Nulsen was treated in a hospital where she embraced the kindness and warmth of the nurses who, she recalls, listened to her and wanted to know how she felt, which subsequently led to a positive outcome. In Karen's case, there is little if any indication that she shared as openly as she could have—and should have—with anyone at all.

Nevertheless, Karen's skeletal appearance toward the end of the 1970s escaped no one. Both Paul Williams and Petula Clark commented on it in broadcast interviews, Williams saying that "I suspected something was wrong. She was so terribly thin. So terribly thin," and Clark recalling the warning she had given to Karen: "I don't know what you're doing, but stop it."

In October 1981, Richard and Karen were interviewed in London by Sue Lawley on a BBC show called Nationwide, and Lawley brought up the rumors swirling around that Karen was suffering from anorexia nervosa, which the host referred to as the "slimmer's disease." Karen denied it. Then, when Lawley attached a number to the rumored weight of her guest—84 pounds—Karen's face took on the look of an angry defendant and she snapped, "No! No!" Her gaunt face and contemptuous eye-rolling didn't help. In a way, it presented to the British public—and now, thanks to the Internet, the rest of the world—the least likeable Karen Carpenter of all time.

"She was used to medications of all sorts," Levenkron said to *A Current Affair* correspondent Mary Garofalo. "The family used a lot of medications to calm anxieties. This was an anxious family."

He further stated that for the entire time Karen was in his care in New York, no one in the Carpenter family called to inquire about her progress. He said he had never had an anorexia patient whose family did not call frequently for updates—that it is common during treatment for anorexia for families to be centrally involved. When the family did visit once, Levenkron asked them all to tell Karen that they loved her, believing that would be a valuable stepping stone. As the story goes, Richard said it without hesitation, but Agnes was unable to utter the words, claiming theirs was not a family that did such things.

At that same meeting, Karen apologized to her family for ruining their lives.

Delving into Karen's relationship with Agnes can spark countless and strident theories, assessments and debates. Through the years, thanks to various articles, reports, reminiscences, rumors, and the facts many are based on, Agnes has been vilified for what certainly appears to be a cold and controlling personality. It is quite easy, then, to accept that Karen was in some ways detrimentally affected by it. In addition to the stories of how she favored Richard, there are many that establish Agnes as one who lacked gentility in expressing her opinions, which were often raw, who had no compunction about voicing her prejudices, which were always baseless, and who could be unsympathetic to Karen and sometimes even to Richard when certain problems or issues arose.

The public saw Agnes and her husband Harold less than a handful of times while Karen was still alive, such as on an episode of *This is Your Life* in 1971 and on the 1978 television special, *The*

Carpenters: A Christmas Portrait. Although all other appearances of Agnes and Harold were fairly ordinary, what stood out on *This Is Your Life* was how embarrassed Agnes made both Richard and Karen feel when she and her husband were called out on stage to surprise their children. It was certainly inadvertent, but telling nonetheless. First, Agnes mentioned "Kathy, What a Chassis," a song that Richard had written when he was a boy, which made Richard, a serious composer, wince in humiliation; then she presented her daughter with the baseball mitt that Karen had used years earlier, which Karen—who was eagerly trying to cast off the tomboy image—instantly hid behind her while trying to hide her mortified expression.

Many of Karen's friends and associates who knew the parents called Harold a sweetheart, for he had a pleasant and genial demeanor. At the same time, many in the musical entourage called Agnes the Dragon Lady because of how she inserted herself into her children's career with opinions and demands that weren't always sensible or sensitive. But Karen, true to her own character, remained devoted to her, and always sought her approval. The night before she died, Karen slept over her parents' house to go shopping with her mother the next day, and as she did while she had still been living at home a few years before, she helped set up breakfast for her mom and dad as soon as she woke that morning.

She was always a good daughter.

(Agnes does indeed come out smelling like anything but roses in the growing volume of Carpenter scholarship. Hardly anyone dares lobby against it, but one thing that should be stressed is that Agnes and Harold took the initiative to purchase several instruments when their children showed interest and talent, including pianos and drums, even though they could barely afford to do so with the family's modest, pre-stardom income.)

Less than two years after Richard and Karen signed on with A&M Records, they were famous around the globe, incredibly rich, and able to write their own tickets for what they wanted to do, where they wanted to go, and how they wanted to live their lives. Karen's issues, however, were obstacles that kept her from taking as much pleasure or gratification from all that as she should have been able to. The pressure of nonstop recording and touring didn't help, denying her a social life of any real enjoyment at all. Sometimes needlepoint, videotapes of old TV programs, and iced tea—her favorite drink—were all she had to sooth her frayed nerves. While there was never any question that she enjoyed making music and was appreciative of the millions of fans who made the Carpenters famous, it is also true that she was overworked with tours and promotion, underwhelmed with the perks of success, and confused about her place in the world.

What made that difficult for others to recognize at the time was that she put on a good face. Rarely in public or even private discourse did she delve into the darkness, but concentrated instead on the predictable and the humorous. Typical of this was a throwaway line on *The Tonight Show* in 1978, when guest host John Davidson asked about a rigorous and often perplexing tour that included a stop in Germany and an appearance on a German television program. Karen, talking about how terribly confused she was about many of the aspects of the production, quipped, "They agreed on nine outfits, and I thought they wanted me to wear them all at once." For public consumption she joked and tossed off her angst as if it had not been a grueling experience at all. She had a great capacity for doing that.

In many ways, in her twenties she was still a little girl who loved Disneyland and Mickey Mouse toys; the purity and sincerity that went along with that prohibited people from thinking there were too many adult problems lurking beneath the surface.

"She was basically a little girl who wanted a normal life. But you can't be a superstar and have a normal life," said John Adrian, who worked for A&M's London office and dated Karen in the mid 1970s. Adrian, who made the comment in 2014 on a British television talk show called *Lorraine*, also pointed out the paradox that, despite her inability to lead a truly normal life, Karen was nevertheless completely "normal—in the best sense of the word." It was, ultimately, a painful irony.

Richard came to believe that a less grueling schedule would have been a wise thing for Karen's mental health, while also steadfastly maintaining that it wasn't show business and family pressures that contributed to her anorexia or any other serious problem. "I think she would have suffered from the same problems even if she had been a homemaker," he once said.

There may be some truth to that.

One additional irony is that despite the fact that Karen would have fared well by spending more time away from a recording or performing environment, in some ways the recording studio was the perfect place for her: she didn't have to act a certain way; her looks really didn't matter; it was where, because of her proven skill in spinning records into gold, she was given the most respect and consideration.

"When she was alone and safely ensconced in a vocal booth with a microphone and a song, she was really at home," says former A&M publicity director Doug Haverty. Many insiders have, in fact, called Richard and Karen "studio people," convinced that that's where they belonged, much more so than on tour or appearing on television shows or doing interviews.

Both Richard and Karen took their music as seriously if not more so than almost anything else in their lives. While no one states that Richard was difficult to work with, he *was* a perfectionist, and he had the capacity to work longer hours than all those around him. Karen was an exceedingly quick study and was able to accomplish behind the microphone whatever Richard required of her with few if any problems, as well as whatever she wanted to bring to the process on her own accord. She really didn't need to be a perfectionist because most of her first takes were already perfect.

Inside the studio and out, for every gloomy recollection like Hal Blaine's and Neil Sedaka's, both of whom remember Karen as being melancholy more times than not, there are former colleagues and associates who take a completely different stance.

Alan Osmond, of the famous Osmond Brothers, dated Karen a few times and denies ever detecting sadness lurking behind her sunny disposition. "I didn't notice any of that," he emphasizes.

Similarly, Carolyn Arzac, a close friend of the Carpenters' secretary (Arzac lived in an apartment complex called "Only Just Begun" that Richard and Karen owned), says that regardless of what Karen was going through emotionally, or how she may have been abusing her body, she never once let it affect her outward demeanor toward the people she worked with or the people she met. "Karen was a special person," Arzac recalls. "Always down to earth, and always very kind. She had a great sense of humor, and she never forgot anyone, from the man who cut the lawn at her house on Newville Avenue, to the mailman, to the people who just opened doors for her."

Many people who worked at A&M felt the same way.

"One day I stopped into the restroom, and someone was whistling quite well in one of the stalls," shares Ronny Schiff, who in the 1970s was the creative director for A&M's sheet music and songbook division. "I whistle very well, and don't know many other women who do. So I waited to see who it was. It was Karen Carpenter! Afterward, right outside the bathroom, we compared women-whistling-well stories. It was a goofy conversation. Upbeat. I mean, how many people start a conversation about whistling in the bathroom?"

While plenty of former colleagues and associates do not hesitate to share their thoughts and recollections of Karen, many others wish not to divulge the details of their memories or emotions; some of her closest acquaintances have such strong feelings that, even years later, they still can't talk about it very easily.

Actor/singer John Davidson, who appeared with the Carpenters several times on television, says that he has very personal sentiments about Karen that he does not care to reveal. He's not the only one-time associate to refuse to discuss it; there are those who simply cannot, because the emotions get in the way. Herb Alpert, interviewed in 2011 on CBS's *Sunday Morning* show, started to cry when discussing Karen with correspondent Russ Mitchell. Alpert was unable to finish his thoughts, and Mitchell had to go on to another topic.

Such reactions simply underscore the fact that Karen the Consummate Professional was as lovable as Karen the Troubled Soul.

5.
Goody Four-Shoes

"We make Pat Boone look dirty."

-Richard Carpenter in People Weekly, 1976.

The toothsome twosome. The Pepsodent twins. White lace and promises.

No one in the public eye is ever immune from the media's love of clever catchphrases to describe what they need to write about. Sometimes catchphrases give writers a quirky way to turn what could be a bland piece into a spicy one. Other times catchphrases just help sell copies. It can happen even when it's not entirely fair, or when the subject tries desperately to leave the blandness behind. In the case of the Carpenters, it wasn't necessarily always Richard and Karen who perpetuated the goody-goody image; many of the marketing and promotion decisions that were made on their behalf made a tricky image even trickier to deal with, and no matter how many times the two of them told interviewers and reporters about their aversion to that persona, it continued unabated.

A comprehensive profile that *Rolling Stone* magazine ran in 1974 begins with Karen's plea: "We're just normal people." Two years later, Richard admitted that he doubted they would ever be able to shed their "squeaky-clean, milk-drinking image," and added that "We make Pat Boone look dirty."

"It's true: they really are bright and well-scrubbed," said broadcaster Jerry Dunphy about the Carpenters on his short-lived television show, *Jerry Visits*, in 1972. "And their background is as wholesome as a Normal Rockwell painting."

Many of their album covers merely underscored the fact that they were inseparable bookends who smiled whenever they were told to smile, or who were so intertwined as a unit that they were practically inseparable, personally and professionally. As late as 1981, when their *Made in America* LP was released (eleven years after their first hit), the cover image selected for the album was a hand-drawn artistic rendering that shows them as one face split in two, with identical white grins. Even when they are shown with a decidedly pensive and non-toothy look, as on their 1975 *Horizon* album cover, the impression is not much altered: there they are shown standing side by side, overlapping, in the exact same hands-in-back-pockets position. The album titled *A Song for You*, from 1972, features a red cover with the Carpenters' logo as a canopy over a drawing of a heart—an image that even a dissatisfied Richard said made the album look like a gigantic Valentine's Day card.

Dubious cover choices began with their first album, *Offering*, which pictured Karen clutching a bouquet of sunflowers and wearing what unintentionally resembled (because of the lighting and the angle) a frock and a head covering. (She actually wore neither.) When *Offering* was re-released and renamed *Ticket to Ride*, it had a much more sophisticated and palatable picture of a laid-back Richard and Karen on a sailboat. The remaining copies of the original *Offering* album cover were reportedly destroyed by A&M.

The connected-at-the-hip persona that plagued several of their album covers extended to promotional videos, publicity photos, and sometimes, inadvertently, concerts. During a 1972 show in Australia, when Richard was introducing the band, he said, "Last but not least, the little lady behind the drums is my sister, not my wife. You may laugh, but quite a few people still think that Karen and I are married." Karen affected disgust and said, "Oh, yuck!" Not wishing to let that be interpreted as an insult to her brother, she quickly covered her mouth in an expression of remorse for saying it.

Yuck indeed, but did she really need to apologize? The bit may have been funnier and more urbane without that, but having jumped into such an aggressive promotional schedule (at just twenty two years of age), she lacked the time she needed for any kind of professional training or guidance at all. Plus, she was highly reliant on and extremely admiring of Richard—so even some professional guidance may not have helped.

"I really don't think they knew exactly how to market us," Richard once stated, referring to A&M. He added that based on the album covers alone, he found it difficult to blame some critics who disparaged their overly-wholesome image.

Album covers were one thing; television appearances were another.

"When we first did TV early in our careers it was a mistake," Karen told a radio interviewer in 1978. "It was violently mishandled. Our TV exposure was disastrous."

As one example, at the beginning of *The Carpenters Very First Television Special* (1976), Karen pointed to Richard and said "I'm Karen," and then Richard pointed to Karen and said, "And I'm Richard," which seemed to be yet another admission of interchangeability.

(Even the television movie from 1989, *The Karen Carpenter Story*, which Richard as executive producer made sure was as watered-down as possible, didn't mask the profound closeness of the siblings.)

In 1971, just a year after they reached superstardom, the Carpenters hosted a summer replacement series called *Make Your Own Kind of Music* to fill the slot normally taken by *The Don Knotts Show*, which was a short-lived comedy/variety series on NBC. The Carpenters shared their hour with many other regulars, including Al Hirt, Mark Lindsay, the New Doodletown Pipers, and the Patchett and Tarses comedy duo. A running theme through every episode was the presentation of giant alphabet letters that provided clues as to what kind of song, skit, or other piece of business was coming up next. Just six episodes were shot, and while the series did allow Richard and Karen the chance to promote many album cuts that the radio-listening public might never have heard, the skits were silly, the pace lackluster, and the show did little to build a following beyond their existing base of fans, large though it already was.

Richard, Karen, and their band appeared on many other shows, as well, and while most of the programs were trivial and reflected the tenor of the times for network television, they did promote the Carpenters' music, if not much else. After a while it must have seemed as good as it was going to get for them, as far as television exposure was concerned. On *The 5th Dimension Traveling Sunshine Show* (971), a typical joke concerned Richard and Karen's last name. The show made believe that the 5th Dimension pop music group was traveling in a covered wagon to present their entertainment in various locales. When a wheel fell off the covered wagon, one of the members of the quintet said, "What we need is a carpenter . . . I'm going to find some carpenters," after which Richard and Karen instantly appeared to sing "Reason to Believe."

Equally silly, but no less musically valuable, was *The Special London Bridge Special* (1972), which pretended to magically transport a very confused Tom Jones, the famous Welsh crooner, to the reconstructed London Bridge in Arizona State Park. The Carpenters were in good company within all the scripted shenanigans, for sharing the spotlight with them was Kirk Douglas, Lorne Greene, Charlton Heston, and, fresh from her success a few months earlier in the popular movie, *The Summer of '42*, Jennifer O'Neill.

There was an equally sizeable cast of famous characters on the *Olivia Newton-John: Hollywood Nights* special (1980), including Andy Gibb, Toni Tennille, Gene Kelly, Elton John, and Tina Turner. Olivia was, by this time, one of Karen's closest acquaintances, and either Karen performed on the show as a favor to her friend or she simply liked the creative direction the show promised to take. (Or both.) One skit had Karen as part of a group called the Heartaches, along with Olivia and Tina Turner, and they danced in what was essentially a filmed, intimate, though high-energy concert, singing the Eagles' song "Heartache Tonight." Karen truly looked to be in her element. (Richard was not part of the show.)

Other variety programs on which the Carpenters were guests included *The Andy Williams Show*, *The Carol Burnett Show*, *The Mike Douglas Show*, specials hosted by Bob Hope and Perry Como, and others. Karen always seemed to enjoy herself in the requisite skits, and became much more comfortable, confident, and relaxed on the TV stage as the years went by; Richard, by contrast, always looked a little awkward, and as a result, was unconvincing and underwhelming. He has since stated that he didn't take much pleasure in doing these shows. He would have much preferred to have been involved with television productions that concentrated almost entirely on music, which is the only thing with which he felt comfortable.

Karen blossomed with well-written and well-directed comedy and parody that was tailored specifically for her. The same was true for dancing: she proved time after time that she was able to learn choreographic moves quickly and flawlessly. Richard never achieved that kind of on-camera comfort and, even given more time, probably never would have.

As previously noted, it wasn't until 1976 that the Carpenters were finally offered their own television special, and while it still had a bit of shtick and a few unconvincing moments, the writers and producers did endeavor to highlight music above all else. *The Carpenters' Very First Television Special* seemed to have renewed Richard and Karen's faith in the medium, and perhaps allowed them to vent some of the stress and tension they had felt with earlier TV efforts. Even most of the skits were musically oriented. With guests Victor Borge and John Denver, it featured, among other bits, a visual discussion of Richard's love of conducting, a breathless tour-de force showcase of Karen's drumming abilities, and several medleys.

The show may not have come about the way it did without a change in management; by this time their promotion was being handled by Jerry Weintraub, a giant in the industry who had worked with Elvis Presley, Frank Sinatra, Led Zeppelin, Neil Diamond, and many others. Weintraub, who passed away in 2015, was a force to reckon with, a promotional whiz and salesman extraordinaire, a professional to be taken seriously not just by the acts themselves, but by the networks and studios that he approached for one project after another on behalf of his clients. One of his clients, John Denver (who appeared on *The Carpenters' Very First Television Special*), called Weintraub "Mr. Charm," while also noting that Weintraub himself boasted about being able to sell bathing suits in Alaska. Even though Richard seemed determined to set his own course and often stated that he and Karen needed to take decisive charge of their own careers (and in many ways they did), they needed a Mr. Charm—someone who was decisive, strong, and influential. Weintraub knew what he was doing, and knew what the Carpenters needed in order to foster a better and stronger image in the public eye.

He, in turn, brought in Tony and Emmy Award-winning director and choreographer Joe Layton to re-imagine their stage show. Layton had by this time already worked with Barbra Streisand, Joel Grey, Bette Midler, Danny Kaye, and dozens of other stars on Broadway, in concerts, on television, and in motion pictures. He did a marvelous job of shaking up the Carpenters' concert performances by shaking out the rust and loosening the knots. In the first half of the 1970s, Richard had been steadfastly committed to recreating on stage the exact sounds that he and Karen and the band had set down on vinyl—nothing more and nothing less— and that made the stage shows as visually uninspiring as they were musically pure. In addition to many other new touches, Layton had Karen actually walk out into the first few rows of the audience. He was also the one who suggested they do a spoof of the Broadway musical *Grease* during which Richard entered the stage on a motorcycle, wearing a leather jacket.

The Carpenters had a few more specials after Weintraub came onto the scene, including *The Carpenters at Christmas* (1977), *The Carpenters: Space Encounters* (1978), and *The Carpenters: Music,*

Music, Music (1980). Without a doubt, the latter was the kind of television special Richard had always dreamed about, with guest stars such as jazz legend Ella Fitzgerald, popular TV crooner John Davidson, and the backing of Nelson Riddle and his Orchestra. Riddle, a composer, arranger, and orchestrator, was one of the most distinguished bandleaders of the era, having worked with Fitzgerald, Frank Sinatra, Judy Garland, Dean Martin, and dozens of others. He was the kind of professional Richard much preferred to spend time with on a television project.

Karen, though she may have missed the chance to perform some comedy, also was clearly in her element, singing duets with Fitzgerald and Davidson, and singing on her own in a decidedly composed and relaxed manner. While it was undoubtedly hard work, she sailed through.

Interestingly, according to Richard, ABC was not happy with *Music Music Music* for the same reason he was happy with it: because it was devoted almost exclusively to music, with little if any comic relief. He said that ABC likened it to a PBS special.

Through it all—the ups and the downs, the successes and disappointments—Richard and Karen never discounted the importance of promotion, and understood the effect that interviews and television exposure had on the popularity and sales of recorded music. What they didn't realize at first what that there were right ways and wrong, and good ways and bad, of going about it. They clearly could have well used Jerry Weintraub, or someone like him, a few years earlier—a management overseer with the foresight to look beyond the existing image and figure out how to modify it to be more palatable to more people.

Touring, too, was considered a vitally important element of marketing, but it was also the cause of certain other problems; perhaps even skilled management would not have rallied against it in the early days of the Carpenters' reign. After all, touring helps sell records and boost popularity, which the record companies want, and also helps validate what has been accomplished in the recording studio, which is what the artists want.

Richard came to regard their relentless touring in the first few years as extremely troubling and damaging. No one saw at the time how it was going to lead to exhaustion, frayed nerves, and hospitalization. In their first five years as superstars, Richard, Karen, and the band performed nearly 1,000 concerts in the U.S. and abroad. Their concerts *did* promote records and earn money, so A&M likely would not have been eager for them to do any less than they were doing at the time, even if Richard and Karen had requested it. For better or worse, that was simply the business part of the music business.

6.
The Boss

> "Karen held her own with us 'bunch of ruffians,' while remaining a total pro."
>
> *-Liberty DeVitto, drummer on Karen's solo album*

Richard often pushed himself to stay awake long enough to do everything he had to do. This included writing all the arrangements he needed to write, listening to the hundreds of songs that were submitted to him to select from, scratching out plans and ideas for studio work, business investments, and other opportunities, thinking about the future, and much more. All this required more hours than the average person might be able to handle, and it took quite a mental and physical toll on the young musical entrepreneur. Although he didn't want to waste too many hours sleeping, he had to sleep. But when he tried to sleep, he wasn't able to.

Agnes had a prescription for Quaaludes which, at the time, was a fairly common sedative. Noticing the state of sleepless anxiety her son seemed constantly to be in, she offered him some of her pills. This began as early as 1971, and several years later, still popping the Quaaludes, Richard realized he had developed an addiction that had the opposite effect of the one intended: he was clearly unhinged and falling apart, not restful and relaxed, as he'd have preferred. His dependence on the drug, combined with the emotional state that goes along with an addiction and his natural urge to be seen as living a perfectly normal life, created in him the kind of devious, cunning behavior that he and many others later associated with Karen, who schemed and conspired when it came to laxatives, thyroid medication, and purging.

In 1978, Richard went to a rehabilitation facility for six weeks, and then decided to take almost an entire year off from the music business.

During Richard's hiatus, Karen decided to embark on a solo project. Her stated goal was not to leave the Carpenters, but simply to add a new dimension to her career. In principle, it was not an entirely foreign concept to Richard, for even he had commented from time to time on his notion to one day explore such ideas as scoring a movie or producing records for other artists. Despite this, Richard admitted to feeling a little bit overlooked and abandoned when Karen discussed her desire to do a solo album. He also felt threatened that she would tether herself, however provisionally, to another producer who would oversee everything from song selections and arrangements to recording techniques and daily scheduling—all things Richard used to handle. At the same time, however, he understood how much his sister craved a spotlight of her very own.

Agnes, however, was by most accounts disturbed by the thought of it. Her vision, from the time her son was a preteen musical prodigy, had Richard at the epicenter of all musical endeavors that revolved around the Carpenter family.

Once Richard gave Karen his blessing to launch a solo project (she said she would not have done so without his okay), she traveled to New York in May 1979 to plan, rehearse, and cut a record that was to have been called *Karen Carpenter*. Her producer was the legendary Phil Ramone, who already had a sterling career, having worked with Ray Charles, Aretha Franklin, Chicago, Paul Simon, Billy Joel, and many others on extremely successful and well-received albums. (Ramone passed away in 2013.)

Deciding to do a solo album was by far the most decisive thing Karen had ever attempted on her own—something she sorely needed to do to build some self-esteem. She came into the project with a great amount of hope, excitement, and commitment.

Although it was not one of her declared objectives—and it may not even have been a conscious idea—the project also gave her a chance to be in charge, really for the first time, of her own life, personally and professionally. Just how much personal and professional satisfaction she was able to claim at the time will always be in doubt.

As far as her personal behavior was concerned, she was abusing laxatives for perhaps the entire time she was in New York. When Karen stayed with Ramone and his wife at their home they found the laxatives hidden in various places near where Karen slept, and one night found her passed out on their kitchen floor. As far as the professional venture was concerned, it was ultimately rejected by Richard, Alpert, and Moss back in California. While it was Ramone who presented Karen with most of the song options for the solo album and tried to sway her one way or another, Karen made the final decisions. Arguably (though devoted fans might disagree), some of the selections proved not have been in her best interest, given her established vocal strengths and the musical styles that fit her somewhat better than others.

What did fit, however, was her presence in the recording studio. According to those who were there during the New York sessions, she was entirely delightful to work with, whether the microphone was on or off, easily and effectively merging both a professional and personable demeanor. Although she rarely if ever socialized with band and production personnel when the sessions concluded each day (other than with Ramone and his wife), she got along with everyone, and everyone got along with her. This is especially notable in light of the fact that Ramone did not necessarily hold back on his taskmaster's role. He was trying to win her over to the idea that this was a project that required a brand new style, substance and personality than she was used to, and sometimes he had to admonish her to get the point across.

"She was going through a lot at the time," recalls Liberty DeVitto, who played drums during the solo sessions, "but it didn't interfere with her professionalism. In a *New York Times* article, our backup band, which was also Billy Joel's band, was called a bunch of ruffians—but Karen held her own with us 'bunch of ruffians' while remaining a total pro."

Guitarist Russell Javors told Billy Joel biographer Mark Bego that although he and his band-mates could sense there were personal problems with which Karen was dealing at the time, she was always entirely friendly. "She was very precise and she had a way that she wanted to do things. But she was a very nice person," he said. "I liked her, and I am sorry that I didn't get to be friends with her. It's one of those bittersweet memories."

"We all loved her and had great respect for her, so were tough on her, but also treated her like a sister, or at least like one of us," DeVitto adds. "She was very gentle, but she did get mad at me once—when I defaced the cover of a Carpenters Christmas album. She scolded me for that."

The song selection for *Karen Carpenter* was far more erotically suggestive than anything Karen had done before as part of the Carpenters. That was one of the points that Karen and Phil Ramone wanted to make—that she was a woman who was independent, shrewd, and sexual. That, of course, was as close to the antithesis as one could get of how a large segment of the public viewed her at the time. DeVitto joked about it during one recording session when they were working on a song called "Make Believe It's Your First Time." The title line is followed with the lyric, ". . . and I'll make believe it's mine." "Right before we began rolling tape one day," De-Vitto recalls, "with Karen listening in the booth, I said out loud that the line should be, 'Make believe it's your first time, and I'll *guarantee* it's mine.' We all busted out laughing, including Karen, and the session had to be delayed. Everyone had the same thought about Karen, but I happened to be the one who said it."

Other songs from those sessions included "Making Love in the Afternoon," "Remember When Lovin' Took All Night," and "My Body Keeps Changing My Mind."

Javors, who wrote two songs selected for the album, including one called "Still in Love With You," once recalled that he had read in the press how Agnes "freaked out" when she heard the first line of the song: "I remember the first time I laid more than eyes on you."

From all accounts, Karen was both at ease and in control in the studio, and confidently accepted her responsibility as the accountable center of attention and the person in charge (a role she shared with Ramone). That was good for her sense of worth, as was the feeling she certainly must have had that many of the men with whom she was working were attracted to her. Indeed, several were, but as DeVitto recalls, that didn't get in the way of boys being boys in front of her.

"For example," DeVitto recalls, "we were in the studio on my birthday, and Phil Ramone went to an 'erotic bakery' to get a cake in the shape of a penis, with my name on it, and there were two little drums at the bottom, which were the testicles, on which Happy Birthday was written. We had a lot of fun with that cake—and Karen was a real sport about it." For the girl from New Haven—now a woman from Downey—spending dozens of hours with the ruffians from Billy Joel's band presented no problem at all, regardless of indelicate jokes and erotically shaped cakes.

Those rehearsal and recording sessions in New York must have been quite interesting for Karen, mixing as they did the fresh pursuit of a feminine mystique with her traditional one-of-the-boys disposition—a demeanor that sprang from her not-too-distant past. After all, the vast majority of the Carpenters' entourage were men, and for a time, not too long after her childhood tomboy days were over, she was lugging and schlepping suitcases and musical equipment with the strongest of them.

In the end, though, the album they put together is generally regarded as being only marginally successful in presenting a new and engaging musical milieu from a new and different Karen Carpenter. When she had first approached her brother about the project, he asked her to please avoid doing any disco music, and while most of the selections on *Karen Carpenter* are not disco, some are; validating Richard's loathing, those are the least appealing cuts. The few light jazz and contemporary fusion numbers in the mix are far more compelling.

"If We Try" was arguably one of the most hit-worthy songs on the album. It used Karen's low-register to good effect, and was also musically in synch with the times without resorting to the era's more annoying musical signatures, such as electronic rhythm sections and ponderous back beats. "If We Try" is the song that artist and videographer Chris Tassin, a major force in the unofficial Karen Carpenter revival of the last few years, uses as the soundtrack for a fascinating, thought-provoking YouTube video about the solo project. The video imagines that *Karen Carpenter* was released when it was supposed to be, and that a retail shop in an upscale mall devoted its entire in-store decor to promoting the album.

When the New York sessions were over, Karen and producer Phil Ramone flew to the A&M studio in California to play the tape for Richard and studio heads Herb Alpert and Jerry Moss. They deemed *Karen Carpenter* not nearly as polished an effort as what they were all accustomed to and hoping for at the label. Some songs merely sounded uninspired to them. Very few of the cuts utilized Karen's lower register, which was always a big part of her appeal. When her upper register was used for songs that lacked decisive hooks (which were many of them), the results were merely common. That was certainly a concern for Richard, Alpert and Moss, all of whom knew that as part of the Carpenters, Karen was always considerably *uncommon*.

After Richard and the top brass at A&M decided to shelve the album, Ramone tried to convince them to listen to it once again, reportedly at the home of Quincy Jones, probably as a way of getting the opinion of someone Richard and the A&M heads would respect unconditionally. Although they also respected Ramone, his involvement *was* conditional: he was trying to please Karen and, at the same time, tap into something that might be more in tune with the times. Richard, Alpert and Moss were more interested in maintaining the elements that made a Carpenters record a Carpenters record, and since A&M was to manufacture and distribute it, they had the clout to stick to that position.

Lyricist John Bettis said that when Richard listened to the playback of the Ramone-produced tracks, he was listening to the world's most distinctive vocalist imitating other vocalists, and just didn't think it was a good idea. Fully aware that there has been controversy since 1980 about the decision not to release the album (most of it pro-Karen and anti-Richard), Bettis reiterated what he knew Richard believed, and perhaps what he believed, as well: "You know why the album was shelved? It wasn't good enough."

Herb Alpert said that he believed even Karen was unhappy with the album, but Ramone's recollection disputes that claim. He said that she told him she was enormously proud of it. It is very possible that Karen, who did not like conflict and cared perhaps a bit too much about what other people thought, went along with the decision to shelve the project simply to avoid a protracted and emotional quarrel.

Richard finally released *Karen Carpenter* in 1996, mostly because of fan pressure. "Not all of it works," wrote Jean Rosenbluth in the *Los Angeles Times* shortly after its official release, "but the country-tinged 'All Because of You' and the shimmering power-poppy 'Making Love in the Afternoon' demonstrate the singer's underutilized versatility."

That encouraging review was written in the present tense, although the era of Karen Carpenter was already thirteen years in the past.

7.
Harmless Oblivion

"The Carpenters: They've Only Just Begun—To Grow Up."

-Title of a 1976 People Weekly *cover story*

One day in 1976, Karen stood behind the microphone at A&M to lay down a track that she'd eventually name her favorite Carpenters song. It was called "I Need to Be in Love," co-written and arranged by Richard for their seventh studio album, *A Kind of Hush.* As time would show, the album didn't burn up the charts. The title track, "There's a Kind of Hush (All Over the World)," first popularized nine years earlier by Herman's Hermits, reached #12 on the singles charts, and "I Need to Be in Love" peaked at #25. The third single from the album, "Goofus," didn't even break the Top 50.

Despite a few personal bumps in the road, Richard and Karen were still willing to record and promote as much music as they could, but as time would show, there were no more #1 hits after that, none in the Top 10, and only one in the Top 20—1981's "Touch Me When We're Dancing."

After *A Kind of Hush,* the three albums Richard and Karen made together had plenty of Carpenter assets, but less of the magnetism and marketability of years past—not because they had changed, but perhaps because they didn't change enough.

Professional artists who are on top of the world for six or seven years should feel fortunate and not necessarily ill-fortuned. Styles and tastes change, along with new generations and national moods. Even many fervent fans of particular musical genres know that they themselves are mere mortals who might miss out on something good if they don't at least explore new avenues and leave old ones behind. Once they no longer sell in the millions, talented artists like the Carpenters can always find ways to make the rest of their careers meaningful and fulfilling, both for themselves and their audience. Richard and Karen, had they chosen to, may have discovered a successful new way in the years to come. The overall image that had dogged the Carpenters since the start may finally have been wearing down some of the fans in the second half of the 1970s who *did* wish to explore other styles from other artists. AM radio featured quite a mixed bag to select from at that time, from disco ("Disco Lady" by Johnny Taylor, "December, 1963," by the Four Seasons, "Love Machine, Pt. 1" by the Miracles, and "A Fifth of Beethoven" by Walter Murphy & the Big Apple Band), to new tunes by popular old standbys ("Silly Love Songs" by Paul McCartney and Wings, and "50 Ways to Leave Your Lover" by Paul Simon), and all the way to pop, funk, and soul ("Love is Alive" by Gary Wright and "Kiss and Say Goodbye" by the Manhattans). The top albums that year came from such diverse acts as Peter Frampton, Fleetwood Mac, Queen, the Eagles, Chicago, Bob Dylan, and Earth, Wind & Fire. Those who did purchase the Carpenters' 1976 and 1977 albums, *A Kind of Hush* and *Passage*, found songs that bore a resemblance to certain other popular alternatives of the day, but many people still regarded them as the same old Carpenters. It just wasn't enough to keep up the momentum of the past few years.

"Popular music in America was changing, but the Carpenters were still identified with conservative America," notes studio engineer Tommy Vicari, who was employed at A&M from 1970 to 1974 and worked there as an independent engineer for several years after that. "In a way, they were still two kids from Downey and didn't seem willing to give that up—even though everyone at the studio still believed in them and they were still making records that sounded amazing."

Richard and Karen continued to struggle with a way to bridge the gap, musically, between the anxiety of the late 1960s and what was turning out to be a kind of triteness of the late 1970s. It was not easy.

The market slide did concern Richard and Karen, and before long it began to worry Jerry Moss of A&M, as well. About *A Kind of Hush*, Richard has stated that his Quaalude addition was at its zenith at the time he and Karen were making it, and he blamed the album's second-rate song selection on that. Among the words and phrases used by reviewers and commentators to describe *A Kind of Hush* were 'bland' and 'too similar to everything else.' In addition to the title tune, it featured such cuts as another oldie remake, Neil Sedaka's "Breaking Up Is Hard to Do," a relatively bland entry called "Boat to Sail," and "Goofus," which was more suited to a TV variety show sketch. There were, of course, some perfectly enjoyable selections, including two Richard Carpenter/ John Bettis originals, "Sandy," which had Karen's confident vocals and Richard's interesting harmonies, and "I Need to Be in Love," in which both Karen and Bettis believed strongly because of its biographical authenticity and the emotion that went along with it.

The next year's *Passage* album, however, had no Carpenter/ Bettis originals, which might be considered one of its problems. Jerry Moss spoke to Richard about the group's downward trend. Richard, in turn, who was tired, anxious, and distracted, said he'd be more than willing to turn over the role of producer (a function he had been taking on for years) to someone else, but there were no takers, leading him to speculate that no one wanted the pressure of following him in the job. He also stated that by this time, in terms of the hit potential of singles, radio programmers were decidedly less friendly to and accepting of the Carpenters than they had been in the past.

Passage features perhaps the most curious selection of songs up to that time, including a calypso number originally covered by Harry Belafonte called "Man Smart, Woman Smarter," the Broadway show tune "Don't Cry for Me, Argentina" from *Evita*, and "Calling Occupants of Interplanetary Craft (The Recognized Anthem of World Contact Day)." This was a seven-minute remake of a song by the Canadian group Klaatu, for which more than a hundred orchestra musicians and fifty background singers were used. The song is led off by a fabricated radio conversation between an effervescent disk jockey (voiced by the band's guitarist, Tony Peluso) and a representative from an unnamed extraterrestrial race.

As always, though, some selections on *Passage* still stand the test of time in terms of agreeability, particularly the two other songs that, like "Calling Occupants," were released as singles: the up-tempo country song "Sweet, Sweet Smile" (which reached #44) and "All You Get From Love Is a Love Song" (#35). But for those two cuts, the days of surefire hits by the Carpenters were, for the most part, long gone.

Jerry Weintraub came into the picture just as the *Kind of Hush* and *Passage* albums were being planned. The shifting musical tenor of the times, however, along with the weariness of the Carpenters' unshakable image and the fact that the Weintraub-related touches had not yet taken effect, may also have played into their lackluster sales and flagging popularity. So did Richard and Karen's personal problems. By 1980 they finally found a television format that worked well for them and with which Richard was imminently comfortable (1980's *Music, Music, Music*). But once again, it suffered from belated timing.

To their ardent fans from yesterday, today, and all the years in between, the fact that a decline is mentioned at all is an almost absurd scenario; after all, Richard had never lost his gift as a supremely talented and intuitive arranger, instrumentalist, and producer, and Karen's vocal gift never wavered. It remained incomparable in its precision even all through the waning (and anorexic) years. Still, chart numbers, the studio's concern, and even their own comments were decisive indicators that the magic of the first few years was gone.

The Carpenters would record three more albums together after *Passage*, including *Christmas Portrait*. Richard's contribution

Setting the stage: promotional glossies from A&M Records

Superstars made in America (courtesy the Brazilian Carpenters Friends Club)

*From Japan
with love: album
advertisements*

At home and at ease (courtesy Carolyn Arzac)

A Christmas pose with father Harold (courtesy Carolyn Arzac)

Loyalty personified: Karen and her secretary Evelyn Wallace
(courtesy Carolyn Arzac)

Road ode (source unknown)

*Day after
day (source
unknown)*

No place to hide away (source unknown)

Genuine smiles, for all we know (source unknown)

Michelle Berting Brett pays tribute in a show called We've Only Just Begun (courtesy Mark Brett and Michelle Berting Brett)

Pam Zeitler takes center stage in The Carpenters Tribute Show (courtesy Pam & Rodd Zeitler)

Michelle Whited gets close to Karen as the star of the tribute show Close to You (courtesy Michelle Whited)

to *Christmas Portrait*, however, was relegated to selecting the material, playing the keyboards (along with popular jazz pianist Pete Jolly), producing the sessions, and a few other tasks; because of the problem he was having with Quaaludes, he felt he was not up to putting his fingers into nearly every aspect of the production, as he had on every previous album. Instead, he hired two renowned veterans in the world of composing, arranging, and conducting, Britain's Peter Knight and America's Billy May, to write the orchestrations for the majority of songs. The sessions for "Christmas Portrait" also feature a large first-rate orchestra and chorus. The resulting album did extremely well, eventually passing more than 14 million units in sales.

Because of his diminished role on the project, Richard once referred to *Christmas Portrait* as Karen's *true* first solo album. As much as she adored her brother, Karen adored Christmas songs with almost equal fervor, and making *Christmas Portrait* was at least one dream that came true for her. Her delight in doing it was evident not just on the album itself, but also in the media chats she had to promote it. "My feeling when the interview was over," said FM100's Carl Goldman, "was that Karen felt as if she and Richard had created a masterpiece. Richard may have selected the material, decided on the order, and helped put it all together, but the songs were definitely her little babies."

Two and a half years later, they produced the *Made in America* album, which gave the Carpenters their final Top 20 hit, "Touch Me When We're Dancing." The album featured a few numbers that spoke to an ongoing musical maturity that showed their combined strength in the recording studio. "I Believe You" was among them. Curiously, though, "I Believe You," when released as a single, reached only #68. Nevertheless, they soldiered on as skilled and resilient leaders of an equally skilled and resilient band.

8.
Mrs. Karen Something-or-Other

"And if you're only using me to feed your fantasy, you're really not in love, so let me go, I must be free."
—*from the song "Love Me for What I Am," on the album* Horizon

Karen was a troubled soul who craved a soul mate.

Dating was one of her greatest challenges. "She once described to me how bad she felt whenever she would go out on a date, and all the attention would be focused on her, not on the guy, everywhere they went," says nationally syndicated disc jockey Charlie Tuna, who interviewed Karen many times on the air. "Inevitably the guy was intimidated, and Karen would always end up saying to them, a little forlornly, Hey—it's only me."

She went out with many men over the years, though most of the relationships lacked enduring romance and in a number of cases consisted of just a handful of dates, or less. Mark Harmon was one of the few actors in the exclusive group, the rest mostly being musicians, including Bill Hudson of the Hudson Brothers (father of Kate Hudson); Alan Osmond of the Osmond Brothers; Mike Curb, who in addition to founding and leading the Mike Curb Congregation was also a composer, record company executive, and politician; comedian Steve Martin (who is also a skilled musician); and pop icon Barry Manilow. It has long been rumored that Richard Carpenter sometimes sabotaged Karen's dates, allegedly including one with Steve Martin, saying that he didn't want to lose quality studio time. Karen, it should be noted, was just as demonstrative about Richard's amorous adventures, inserting her opinions and sometimes even her anger when she wasn't comfortable with his romantic choices. We may never know if this was out of pure concern for his decision-making, or if it had something to do with its potential affect on the one constant in her life— the Carpenters.

Karen also dated several men involved with her career on one management level or another, either from her own record label or other companies with which it was associated. Terry Ellis, Jerry Luby, David Alley, and John Adrian are some of the names on that list.

Karen liked Barry Manilow, being able to connect with him both on a musical level and a personal one (for he had plenty of issues of his own). She enjoyed his work. In a March 1977 newspaper column, entertainment writer and radio host Jack O'Brien filed this report: "Barry Manilow took Karen Carpenter to see *A Chorus Line* at the Shubert. They met in Little Rock at one of Barry's concerts, and he visited Karen at hers in Dallas. It's a bloomin' palship already." Of course, it really wasn't. Between their dizzying schedules, her need for family approval, and at least one account that Manilow simply was not interested in her romantically, it was over not long after it began.

She also dated a married man, fellow performer John Davidson, although he was separated at the time. Davidson, with whom Karen appeared on two Carpenters television specials and on *The Tonight Show* when he guest hosted for Johnny Carson, accompanied Karen on a few outings. His on-camera interactions with her, particularly on the TV specials, indicate his distinct fondness. It is very likely that Karen's inherent ability to listen, to understand, and to deny herself any spotlight in the presence of others, prompted Davidson to seek out her comfort during the time of his marital woes. *People Weekly* played down any deep romance by writing that he has ". . . buddily dated singer Karen

Carpenter, who soon will marry wealthy California industrialist Thomas Burris . . . ."

Discovering colleagues who developed a deep affection for Karen is by no means unprecedented. It was almost written on John Denver's face (and in his several butterfly kisses) when he did a few duets with her during the first Carpenters television special in 1976, and drummer Liberty DeVitto has admitted that he fell in love with her during the New York solo sessions. One Carpenters associate from their breakout days, who wishes to remain anonymous, emphatically asserts that Karen always had a sweet and fetching allure, even in the earliest days of their stardom, and that he, too, was smitten by her. It is conceivable that Karen didn't even recognize this and would have been surprised (or at least terribly embarrassed) if told about it.

Cries of "I love you, Karen" were called out numerous times by infatuated fans, and reports of marriage proposals from strangers were not uncommon, some that were shouted out at concerts, others that were sent through the mail. One young man attending a Carpenters concert sat down at Karen's drums during the opening comedy act and punched the policeman who came to pull him away. "Don't touch me," the man growled, "I'm engaged to Karen Carpenter."

Several unsolicited engagement rings also arrived by mail at the Carpenters' Downey home.

Incidents like these naturally made Karen long for a more normal existence. The fact that she was internationally famous and unpretentious at the same time, with modest needs and simple tastes, brought along with it a paradox: she had to be protected and chaperoned everywhere she went, yet exuded an aura of being entirely approachable because of her girl-next-door appearance and persona.

Still, she did speak often of marriage. In a 1978 magazine article she lamented, "Someday I'll be Mrs. Karen Something-or-Other, mother and housewife. Then, I think, I'll be happier than I am now."

As much as she was motivated to keep the Carpenters alive, she was also keenly interested in starting a family. All of her close friends knew how much she adored children and longed to be a mother, but she decided that the father of those children would have be independently wealthy, as a way of ferreting out love interests who would desire her only for her money. He also had to be a maverick, an entrepreneurial type who could easily ignore and flick away the madness of what fame—of what being Mr. Carpenter—would bring to a marriage. As much as Richard tried to micromanage the Carpenters, Karen was trying to micromanage her love life. It didn't work out the way she had hoped.

A few months after the disappointment of the shelved solo album, Karen met and, despite the suspicions and warnings of many people around her, married a handsome and successful real estate developer by the name of Tom Burris. At least he *said* he was a successful real estate developer. Apparently it wasn't true. He went through a large stash of her money and seems to have added to the union no significant earnings of his own.

Burris also neglected to tell Karen about his pre-engagement vasectomy. She cried to her mother that she didn't want go through with the wedding. But Agnes, horrified at the prospect of canceling a lavish ceremony that *People Weekly* was scheduled to attend and cover, told her that since she was responsible for coming this far, she had no choice but to go through with it.

Karen obeyed. Vows were exchanged. The wedding took place on August 31, 1980. *People* covered it two weeks later in photo feature called "Karen Carpenter's All-Star Wedding." Ultimately, the marriage, like the solo album, was shelved.

Upon first meeting her, Burris told Karen that he didn't know who she was and had no knowledge at all about the Carpenters, which seems a little farfetched. That was also the way their first encounter was portrayed in the superficial television movie that aired on CBS in 1989, *The Karen Carpenter Story*, which glosses over both the man and the marriage. Burris was promised what many assume was a small fortune by the Carpenter family to abstain from ever discussing Karen and the marriage. Between his inability to talk about it (he may not even want to if he could) and Richard's highly guarded open dialogue about anything having to do with the Carpenters, the public may never know if there was ever any true love within the relationship, regardless of how brief or fragile.

Nor may we ever know just how much of Karen's own quirks, attitudes, and behaviors may have added to the marital meltdown. Within the world of Karen fandom, any observer who tries to give Burris the tiniest benefit of the doubt swims in treacherous waters, but it would be neither criminal nor unseemly, taking Karen's personal issues into consideration, to suggest that *any* man, even Mr. Truly Perfect, would have had a very difficult time living with her.

Six years before walking down the aisle, the Carpenters recorded a song that could have served as a warning, had Karen known at the time that there was reason to be forewarned. Called "Love Me for What I Am," it was composed by Palma Pascale and John Bettis:

"You've got to love me for what I am
For simply being me
Don't love me for what you intend
Or hope that I will be.

And if you're only using me
To feed your fantasy
You're really not in love
So let me go, I must be free."

It was another one of the many dozens of bittersweet love songs in the Carpenters' musical register that were more bitter than sweet—which, of course, is not an uncommon trend in the world of recorded music. With Karen, however, in romance and beyond, bittersweet was the soundtrack of her life.

Karen lived in three lovelorn versions of catch-22. First, it was her career as the voice of the Carpenters that gave her the greatest validation as a person of high value, personal strength, and meaning, but it was that same career that in many ways stood in the way of turning her most treasured fantasy into reality. Secondly, she assertively pined for love and romance, knowing full well that her family was capable of being equally assertive in undermining it. Finally, while recording and performing gave her the strength and meaning she needed to stay vital, she often spoke as if she would give it all up for the sake of a loving husband and growing family.

Still, one of Karen's dreams did come true, albeit fleetingly: she finally did become a Mrs. Karen Something-or-Other, before that particular dream turned into a nightmare.

9.
All Shook Up

"It's a whole new bag. It's a whole new sound."

-from the Carpenters' Morton's Potato Chips commercial

There are decades worth of chronicles that show how Karen lived anything but a tedious and trivial life. While it may fall short of being called scandalous, her life was nevertheless full of surprises, with personal and professional tales that were at times strange, amusing, and surprising. No one knows them all, simply because not all have yet to be uncovered, but the ones that *are* known paint an interesting and complex picture. After all, within those tales flow such diverse personalities as Elvis Presley, Kenny Rogers, and John Wayne, such extracurricular activities as appearing on *The Dating Game* and shooting TV commercials for snack foods, and the kind of emotional upheavals that a sensitive person like Karen would experience when friends and colleagues are fired or file lawsuits.

Indeed, it was a colorful palette that began even before she was signed to a solo recording contract at sixteen years of age, continued through her first stab at independence (by moving in with her brother to a house not far from their parents'), and lasted well beyond a honeymoon that she really didn't want to go on.

Karen idolized Richard and spent plenty of time with him listening to records, but a fast-forward review of her childhood would emphasize just how much time she spent without him—running bases, catching passes, even shooting make-believe machine guns. Such a review would also reveal how confusing it must have been to deal with a mother who was known to make intolerant comments about Jews and Blacks. It would emphasize Karen's bumpy journey to proficiency on the drums, only because before the drums she tried and ultimately gave up on several other instruments, including the flute, accordion, and glockenspiel.

Most people regard the beginning of the Carpenters as the time when "(They Long to Be) Close to You" first hit the airwaves and quickly became a hit. In one respect that's true, though it wasn't really the beginning at all. Their rise was not overnight; they toiled for several years before that in one musical incarnation or another, thanks mostly to Richard's tireless efforts. One of the most interesting parts of that toil is the fact that it was Karen who was offered a recording contract first, to be a singer for Magic Lamp Records. Richard was signed a few days later as a songwriter with the company's publishing arm, apparently to keep peace in the Carpenter family: it was clear to just about everyone at the time that Agnes was far more interested in Richard's future as a musician, not necessarily Karen's.

The fact that Karen and not Richard was the one first singled out for a contract—by the label's founder and owner, Joe Osborn, who sensed something special about her voice—must have presented a somewhat delicate internal quandary for Karen. After all, she must have been sensitive to the fact that it was Richard's obsession and skill that was responsible for Osborn hearing her sing in the first place. How the principal signing of Karen to the label affected her relationship not just with her brother, but also with their mother, was probably a predicament with which she had to deal on a daily basis.

In a way, it may have been providential for the Carpenter family dynamic that Magic Lamp Records was forced to fold a year later due to a lack of funds for marketing and promotion. Had it not, and had Karen Carpenter become a solo recording star—even a minor one—that family dynamic might have exploded in ways one can only imagine. (Karen did record a single for the small independent label, with a song written and arranged by Richard, called "Looking for Love." Only 500 45-rpm discs were pressed, and today copies in usable condition sell for as much as $2,500.)

Even while Richard began experimenting with the multi-layered vocals that would soon come to be identified as the Carpenters' sound, and even though they were confident that their combined skill and unique style would lead them to some sort of professional launching pad, Karen nevertheless considered other opportunities that came along. At one point, she auditioned for Kenny Rogers to be a singer in his band, the First Edition, and at another point she was asked by John Wayne to try out for the role of Mattie in the movie he was soon to make, *True Grit*.

Kenny Rogers remembers that Karen sang wonderfully at the audition, but didn't feel her voice would blend well with the style he was after. He eventually chose Mary Arnold, a singer originally from Iowa, dark haired and petite like Karen, who had been the roommate of the First Edition's original female vocalist, Thelma Camacho. Arnold stayed with the group until 1975, the year before Rogers embarked on a solo career.

In the summer of 1968, John Wayne was a celebrity judge on *Your All-American College Show* on an episode in which the Richard Carpenter Trio appeared. Karen was eighteen. The syndicated television program, emceed by Dennis James, who by then was already a well-known TV announcer and game show host, featured three celebrity judges on each episode from the world of entertainment, such as Arthur Godfrey, Rose Marie, Bill Bixby, Tammy Grimes, Ryan O'Neal, and others. When Wayne was a judge, he saw in Karen's singing and drumming the kind of energetic hardiness that was fitting for the character of Mattie in *True Grit*, and recommended her to the filmmakers. They, however, wanted someone who already had acting experience. The role of the fourteen-year-old Mattie eventually went to twenty-one-year-old Kim Darby—another dark-haired and petite young woman— who had already appeared in dozens of television shows, including *Mr. Novak, The Fugitive, The Donna Reed Show, Bonanza,* and *Star Trek.*

One interesting trek the simblings made, right after "Close to You" was released and while they were still living at their parents' house, may have been as promotional as it was personal. They appeared on the popular television show, *The Dating Game.* Karen was the bachelorette who had to select one of three bachelors in the first game of the episode, and Richard was one of three bachelor choices to be selected by a young bachelorette in the second. The winning couples would go on an all-expense-paid chaperoned date to a vacation destination either in the U.S. or abroad.

The promotional element came in the form of their performance of "(They Long to Be) Close to You" at the opening of the show, further supported by host Jim Lange mentioning their first pre-stardom album, *Offering.* The personal element may or may not have ever been realized. Karen selected a young man from England, who was mentioned as being in "the beauty world," and who enjoyed cars, horseback riding, and tennis. The location of their date was supposed to have been Washington, D.C. and Roanoke, Virginia. Richard selected a young woman who was an executive secretary, computer programmer, and scuba diver, and their trip was planned for San Francisco. As the announcer said during the closing credits, "Dates with celebrities are always subject to their availability," and it was just about the time of the airing of the show that the Carpenters ceased having anything resembling a personal life. Their days were spent recording, promoting, and touring, and no record exists of the dates having been fulfilled.

Richard and Karen, still so young and inexperienced on TV, must have felt somewhat at home on *The Dating Game* set since so many of their mentor's songs were used throughout the show. "Spanish Flea," "Whipped Cream," and "Lollipops and Roses," all recorded by Herb Alpert and the Tijuana Brass, opened and closed various segments of the series week after week. Which brings up another intriguing unknown that could have shaken things up from time to time: if Agnes was as prejudiced as the tales indicate, her children must have lived with a certain amount of perpetual anxiety based solely on the fact that so many people involved with the Carpenters through the years were Jewish, including Herb Alpert, Jerry Moss, Burt Bacharach, Hal David, Jerry Weintraub, and many others.

Throughout their active years as the Carpenters, what Richard and Karen promoted exclusively was their music—except for a handful of times when they promoted merchandise that had nothing to do with records, tours, or TV appearances. Morton's Potato Chips, High Crown Milk Chocolate, and Suntory Pop were three products for which Richard and Karen filmed television commercials and recorded jingle music. The product marketing and advertising people made sure to link the young-at-heart, easygoing style of the Carpenters' music and appearance with the youthful, carefree characteristics of the products they were selling.

Morton's, which was owned by General Mills, was headquartered in Dallas, and the product was popular mostly in Texas, though the Carpenters recorded the jingle and filmed the spot in Toronto during a break in one of their Canadian tours. Both the High Crown Milk Chocolate and Suntory Pop soda commercials were for Japanese consumers only, and it was only there—where the Carpenters were always grandly celebrated—that the commercials aired on television.

There are other surprises in the Carpenters' non-musical almanac, as well, such as the fact that Karen was plucky enough to dance around on stage pretending to have ice-cream cone breasts under her blouse, and naïve enough not to know that Elvis Presley was trying to get her into a carnal *ménage-à-trois*.

Relatively introverted (and not very busty), Karen initiated campy bosomhood in a musical setting ten years before Madonna did it in her own famous music video. Beginning in 1976, thanks to the intervention of new management and a new stage director and choreographer, the Carpenters included in their live show a spoof of the Broadway musical *Grease*, which had not yet been made into a movie. During the bit, Karen had colossal conical cups under her blouse and camped it up while singing about a virginal life in the song "Look at Me, I'm Sandra Dee." Fans even modestly familiar with her typical stage persona might have been enormously surprised to see it. In the vast majority of stage performances, Karen was far more reserved, even somewhat inhibited. This was a major departure.

The Elvis incident had been related by her friend, singer Petula Clark, first on a Karen Carpenter fan website and then again in 2012 on the Australian morning television show, *Today*. As Clark tells it, one night she and Karen went to see Presley perform. They visited his dressing room after the show, which was initially packed with members of his entourage, but emptied quickly so that just the three of them were left. According to Clark, Elvis's intention was clear, and it had the words 'sexual threesome' written all over it. Over the years, Elvis had successfully plied his charms on a string of alluring ladies, such as Ann-Margret, Juliet Prowse, Connie Stevens, and Natalie Wood. Feeling as if she needed to be an older sister to Karen, Clark indicated in no uncertain terms that it was time to leave, but Karen had no idea why her friend wanted to depart so quickly and practically had to be dragged out. She never grasped what Elvis had in mind.

Karen, of course, eventually found her own would-be king, the handsome and charismatic Tom Burris, who she agreed to marry despite the fact that he had lied to her and withheld important truths, and that several of her friends and associates warned her that something about him seemed terribly awry. To try to make the honeymoon a little more palatable, she invited members of her family, as well as Burris's family, to go along with them to Bora Bora. (Author Ray Coleman reported in his 1994 Carpenters biography that Burris's brother and sister-in-law did accompany them.) Karen cut the honeymoon short by several days.

Two episodes within her professional sphere must have been disturbing for her, even though they had nothing to do with her own actions. They were significant only because of the agonizing ways in which she likely reacted to them, considering that she was very sensitive to the feelings and emotions of the people around her. The first episode involved drugs; the second, lawyers.

While many viewed the Carpenters, as a band, more suited for *The Lawrence Welk Show* than *Midnight Special*, there were a large number of distinct individuals and personalities employed in the entourage who would prove otherwise. According to one associate who toured with the group, a member of the touring staff overdosed on heroin after a show one night and had to be rushed to a hospital. Richard, concerned about potential negative publicity, was enraged and fired him that very night.

The legal incident involved someone Karen liked and to whom she was grateful. After several albums on which Jack Daugherty was listed as producer, Richard regarded the credit as somewhat absurd since he had handled most of the producer's duties. He let A&M know of his dissatisfaction with the arrangement, and A&M, in turn, let Daugherty go. In response, Daugherty sued the label. The matter eventually went to court, where A&M prevailed.

How those incidents affected Karen is unrecorded, but her reaction to the firing of Neil Sedaka as the Carpenters' opening act during a 1975 tour *has* been documented. Sedaka fell out of favor with Richard for using the Carpenters' orchestra, inadvertently breaking a string on Richard's piano, and asserting what Richard thought was too much clout on the tour. As a result, Richard canceled all of Sedaka's upcoming appearances on the bill.

"Richard says he fired me because I was introducing celebrities who were in the audience," Sedaka says, acknowledging that headliners do usually assume that role. "But my take on it is that I was getting too much applause and too many good reviews. It's a shame. We were a great double bill." For her part, Karen was extremely upset and expressed regret to Sedaka about the unfortunate turn of events—although there was nothing she could do about it since Richard was more or less running the show.

Karen's proximity to such emotional events must have been disquieting for a young woman who would much rather have been sitting in her bedroom next to her collection of Disney animals.

Speaking of Mickey and Minnie, one of Karen's most endearing personality traits was her devotion to everything Disney, and her Disney connections extended well beyond her dresser and bedspread. It wouldn't be surprising if in some way she put many of those connections in motion, in her own gentle yet determined way. In addition to visiting Disneyland to shoot the video to promote the "Please Mr. Postman" single in 1975, Richard and Karen returned on a number of occasions for such events as a special performance on behalf of the University of Southern California, as part of the Disneyland Silver Anniversary celebration, and on *Walt Disney's Wonderful World of Color* TV show in 1978 for a special episode called "Mickey's 50."

In addition to the stuffed animals, Karen also collected Disney dishware, music boxes, and other items. How thrilled she must have been to have Cubby O'Brien join the Carpenters as a drummer in 1973, for he had been a Mouseketeer on TV's *Mickey Mouse Club* in the late 1950s. O'Brien, four years older than Karen, was also a highly skilled musician. Richard and Karen had met him when they appeared on *The Carol Burnett Show* in 1971, where Cubby was the drummer for the orchestra. Beginning in 1973, and continuing for the next six years, Cubby often played drums for the Carpenters while they toured. A Disney collectible come to life, right there in Karen's entourage.

Karen was nineteen when the Carpenters finally were signed to A&M—barely an adult, but a little more confident as a musician and more professionally assertive than she was during the Magic Lamp stint. The Carpenters had seven Top 10 hits in the first two years, and millions of dollars in income to go along with it. That the hits piled up one after another is a testament to Richard's skill and prescience as a song selector and arranger, to Karen's ability to learn quickly and adapt to almost any professional demand thrown her way, and of course to the quality of her voice, which was already distinctive and instantly identifiable. Other professionals with that amount of success might have used it to build an invigorating and independent lifestyle of their very own. Karen, however, continued to live with her parents for several more years, as did her brother. The first time both finally moved out, it was into a shared house not far from the one they had just left. Still, Karen must have considered it a giant leap forward, based on what she told her one-time boyfriend, A&M's John Adrian: "She sent me a note when she moved away from her parents," he told the host of *Lorraine* on British television, "and she said, 'This bird has finally flown the coop.'" She did—though only by about a mile and a half.

10.
New and Old Horizons

"Weren't they something?"

*-Karen Carpenter, referring to the children who sang with her
at a 1974 concert in Japan*

The Carpenters had millions of fans around the world. Their greatest popularity outside of the United States extended to England, Japan, and Australia, and they also enjoyed much public support and media attention whenever they visited Germany, Scotland, the Philippines, Brazil, Argentina, and many other countries. Top 20 hits overseas were quite common for the group, including nine in Australia, eight in Brazil, seventeen in Canada, and twelve in Ireland. In Japan they had sixteen albums on the Top 20 list (some of which were exclusive to the Japanese market). They had thirteen in England.

In 1971, the Carpenters embarked on their first European tour, including a sell-out concert at England's Royal Albert Hall, which at the time had been hosting luminaries of a decidedly different musical milieu, such as Jimi Hendrix, Cream, Bob Dylan, and Deep Purple. Karen, Richard and the band were welcomed with an enormous amount of anticipation, appreciation and, following their appearances, devoted fandom that continued throughout their active years and to the present day.

In 1976, to make up for a tour they had postponed earlier due to exhaustion, they returned to England and filled every seat at such impressive venues as the London Palladium. So important was the British love affair with the Carpenters that, despite the hectic schedule, they decided to record a live album there and had it mixed and released just days after they left the country.

They performed for 12,000 fans at Tokyo's famed Budokan arena. The first rock band to have performed there was the Beatles, in 1966 (to some controversy). The Carpenters also performed at Festival Hall in Osaka, where Karen sang the famous *Sesame Street* song by written Joe Raposo, "Sing," along with the Kyoto Children's Choir. (On the *Now & Then* album the Jimmy Joyce Children's Choir provided the young voices.) Karen also sang a few lines of "Sing" in Japanese. The single reached #8 on the Japanese record charts. "Jambalaya (On the Bayou)," also from *Now & Then*, was another top-selling single in Japan. At the beginning of a 1974 concert tour there, 5,000 fans showed up at the Tokyo airport when the Carpenters arrived. That's a thousand more fans than met the Beatles when they landed in New York on February 7, 1964.

In 1976, on a rescheduled European tour, they returned to Japan once again to do twenty-one concerts in only twenty-seven days, and each one sold out. At the time, it was the largest-grossing musical tour in Japanese history. Tickets sold out within one hour of going on sale.

Michael Kanert, managing editor of Japan's best-selling English magazine, *Metropolis*, reports that even today, the lyrics of Carpenters songs are sometimes printed in Japanese school textbooks to help teach English.

"Along with ABBA and the Beatles, the Carpenters appear to be among the most beloved foreign bands here, with both the older and younger generations," notes Kanert's colleague, Martin Leroux, editor of *Metropolis*. "There are Carpenters tribute concerts held all over Japan, even in the countryside. I think they're beloved here due to their essence: Japanese culture values innocence and purity, and those are qualities embodied in Karen's angelic and youthful vocals." Leroux adds that in the 1970s, songs about hope were quite popular in Japan, and a typical Carpenters song empowered people to have hope in what he calls a gentle, non-aggressive way, further embodying Japanese values.

Carpenters songs are covered by many artists in Japan, and often these artists interpret the tunes in other musical styles, such as punk and bossa nova. There is also a very popular Carpenters fan club in the country.

In 1972, the Carpenters played at the Chevron Hotel in Sydney, Australia, and at Festival Hall in Melbourne. Many people Down Under refer to Festival Hall as the House of Rock and Roll, as it has hosted the Beatles and several other top musical acts through the years (as well as non-rock icons like Frank Sinatra). In Australia, Karen seemed to be at her most natural and most relaxed while on stage, even compared to some of her American concerts. She clearly had a blast on that tour, gleefully playing the drums and having an obviously enjoyable rapport with band member Doug Strawn while they engaged in several duets.

The Carpenters made just one trip to Brazil, but that one trip, in combination with their air play on Brazilian radio in the 1970s and all the years since, keep them in a national embrace. They are still extremely popular there today. Their trip in November 1981 included two television appearances, several radio interviews, and publicized visits to a popular tourist spot in Rio de Janeiro and shopping centers in Rio and São Paulo. A group called The Brazilian Carpenters Friends Club is active today in the country and hosts an annual Carpenters convention in Rio de Janeiro. A similar group in Argentina, The Carpenters Argentina Fans Club, founded in 1972, also runs many events.

In one of the oddest of ironies, there are two cities, both in the U.S., where unabashed references to the Carpenters' legacy would seem most appropriate, and yet are curiously in short supply. Given their monumental popularity in the early days, public heritage is practically nonexistent in New Haven, Connecticut, where Richard and Karen lived until they were teenagers, and Downey, California, where the family relocated in 1963 and where

Richard and Karen lived until their middle and late twenties, re-spectively.

"They left New Haven with talent, but not with fame," says Lucia Paolella, former principal at the Nathan Hale elementary school where Richard and Karen had been students. That, she specu-lates, may be why there isn't much Carpenters heritage in town. "Someone told me that once there was a plaque in Karen's honor here at school, before we relocated," she adds, "but I haven't been able to find it."

Following a lengthy article that appeared in the *Downey Patriot* on the occasion of the 30th anniversary of Karen's death, one local resident noted in the comments section of the newspaper, "Sadly, nothing is happening here in her hometown . . . Maybe someday Downey will figure out a way to permanently honor the Carpenters, something bigger than the display of gold records in the library." "Why hasn't Downey done anything to honor Karen and Richard? The Carpenters put Downey on the map!" wrote another. "At least a plaque!"

11.
The End of Romance

"You were funny and nice. A little naive. And you lived for your music."

-Petula Clark, in concert at the Royal Albert Hall, February 6, 1983

There are those who say that if Richard and the principals at A&M Records had supported Karen in her effort to make her solo album a reality by releasing it, she would have been contented and assertive enough *not* to have jumped into a marriage with an untrustworthy groom that was doomed before it began. The two events taken together—the failed album and the failed marriage—may have sparked a deep depression from which she never recovered.

To that picture must be added many others of equal anguish from earlier days, when Karen struggled with her brother's elevated position in the family aspirations (and in their mother's eyes), with body issues related both to her self-image and how she felt she had to look to be a superstar, and with sheer exhaustion.

With all those elements lined up in a row, it should come as a surprise to no one that Karen developed habits that eventually turned a baffled and shattered heart into a permanently damaged one. On the other hand, she may have been damaged long before the discarded album and the broken marriage, with deeply-rooted psychological issues from childhood. In public, she almost always had a smile, a quip, a funny face, and sometimes even an outfit adorned with a Disney character. So who would really know?

Karen was finally convinced to enter into therapy with an anorexia specialist in Manhattan because evidently she had had enough scares, including fainting, exhaustion, tour cancellations due to ill health, and reportedly even what was called a mini stroke during which one side of her face went numb. But in the final analysis, Karen's world may not have changed in a significantly positive way—at least not enough—following the New York sessions.

On the night of February 3, 1983, Karen slept over her parents' house, in an upstairs bedroom, so that the next day she and her mother could pick up on the shopping they had begun that afternoon. In the morning, Karen went downstairs and did a little bit of breakfast preparation for herself and her parents, then returned to the upstairs room, presumably to get dressed. Agnes called to her not long afterward to come downstairs. There was no answer; in fact, there was no noise at all—no whimpers, no thumps, nothing. Agnes went upstairs and found Karen on the floor of the walk-in closet, nearly lifeless. There were no bruises on her body, indicating that she collapsed slowly and didn't just drop to the floor following a catastrophic event. The paramedics who arrived shortly after her father's desperate phone call detected a slight pulse. As was later determined, Karen's heart had shrunk because of her previous dramatic weight loss, and its muscle had been eaten away by the Ipecac syrup she frequently ingested to induce vomiting. The final moments of her life were a sluggish yet lingering failure of her heart's ability to keep her alive. She was pronounced dead at Downey Community Hospital.

Television reports that afternoon and evening spread the sad news across the country. "She left us all too soon," announced co-anchor Paul Moyer on Los Angeles's Eyewitness News. "Karen Carpenter, whose soft and mellow voice was known to millions, died in a hospital in Downey this morning of cardiac arrest."

"Singing star Karen Carpenter died today of an apparent heart attack at the age of 32," reported Ted Koppel during an ABC national news brief. "In the past she had suffered from a weight loss condition known as anorexia nervosa."

The following morning, the nation's newspapers took up the task of informing the public coast to coast. "Karen Carpenter, 32, Is Dead; Singer Teamed With Brother," ran the *New York Times* headline; "Seventies Soft-Rock Star Karen Carpenter Is Dead at Age 32," said the *Atlanta Constitution*; "Singer Karen Carpenter, 32, who with her brother, Richard, helped bring romance back to pop music in the 1970s with mellow songs like 'We've Only Just Begun' and 'Close to You,' died of cardiac arrest Friday," wrote the *Chicago Tribune*. Their story was basically a minor variation of the wire-service article issued by United Press International and picked up by dozens of daily newspapers.

One episode of a 2014 British television show called *Autopsy: The Last Hours Of* focuses on the case of Karen Carpenter. In the show, which has scrutinized the deaths of such celebrities as Michael Jackson and Whitney Houston, forensic pathologist Dr. Richard Shepherd conducted a detailed analysis of the actual autopsy report, an analysis that the producers supplemented with interviews by people who knew her, worked with her, or closely followed her career. Shepherd does not rip apart the widely held belief that the anorexia nervosa from which she suffered had weakened her heart to the point of failure, but he, like Levenkron before him, enters into the mix several other elements that merely compound the story and make it even harder to draw any decisive conclusions.

At death, Karen weighed 108 pounds and had a body mass of 18.5, which for a woman of five feet, four inches, was average. Autopsy indicators also suggest that Karen was still menstruating, which most anorexics do not, and that her lungs, liver, and kidneys were all normal, which in anorexics often are not.

Shepherd states that psychologically, at least, Karen was still affected by the issues that turn people into anorexics, which is why she was still taking drugs to induce vomiting. In that way, she had *not* broken free from the disease. Plus, the autopsy found no evidence of any meal Karen might have eaten the night before she died, but *did* find evidence of the Ipecac syrup.

Adding yet another tricky piece to the puzzle is the fact that at the time of her death she had an active prescription to the anti-anxiety medication Ativan. Evidently, she was feeling a significant-enough amount of anxiety to warrant the prescription. Just precisely what she was anxious about at that particular time cannot be entire clear, though the list of suspects is long indeed. The solo album and marriage fiascos were still relatively fresh in her mind. Plus, she was supposed to have signed and delivered the divorce papers the day she died and may have been thinking nervously about her future. Her last recording session had been nine months earlier, and the last Carpenters album had been released more than a year-and-a-half before. In her overwrought mind, she may have been refereeing a nasty bout between career worries and personal dilemmas.

Whatever the need for the anti-anxiety medication, the number of pills left in the bottle, when measured against the original prescription date, indicates that Karen had been taking far fewer than prescribed. Ironically, it may have been the one medication she really needed. Whether or not that had any effect on the sad events of February 3 will never be known.

Karen's funeral was held at the Downey United Methodist Church on Tuesday, February 8, 1983. In addition to the mourners in the sanctuary, which included Olivia Newton-John, Burt Bacharach, Dionne Warwick, Herb Alpert, and other luminaries, approximately 250 people were in an overflow room and another 400 in a courtyard. Reverend Charles Neal from New Haven, Connecticut, delivered the eulogy. The Cal State University Choir sang the "Adoramus Te" hymn (Latin for "We adore thee"). They were under the direction of Richard's former college instructor, Frank Pooler, who was instrumental in Richard's development as an exceptional choral arranger, and who had worked with the Carpenters several times as a conductor. Pallbearers included

Alpert, John Bettis, band member Gary Sims, and several other friends and business associates.

That day and over the next few days, many of Karen's performer friends took a few moments during their own concerts to acknowledge the colleague they already missed terribly. Petula Clark, appearing at London's Royal Albert Hall three days after her death, said of Karen in front of a hushed audience, "You were funny and nice. A little naive. And you lived for your music."

The report of Karen's death was said to have hit Olivia Newton-John extremely hard. She had grown to become one of Karen's closest friends; she and her first husband, actor and dancer Matt Lattanzi, had socialized on a number of occasions with Karen and Tom Burris. Newton-John had a stark reminder of what Karen had gone through twenty years later when it was discovered that her own daughter, Chloe Lattanzi, suffered from anorexia nervosa.

Twenty miles from Karen's hometown of Downey, CA, on the celebrated Hollywood Walk of Fame, a plaque was placed for the Carpenters in recognition of their astounding success. "My only regret is that Karen is not physically here to share it with us," Richard said during the ceremony on October 12, 1983. "It will never be quite the same without Karen, because it was quite an experience working with her."

It was never quite the same at A&M, either, where a lingering sadness lasted long after she was gone. Some say that staffers there had a very hard time talking about Karen, and that it wasn't unusual at all to see tears when they did talk about her. Without exception, Karen had an overwhelming impact on everyone who knew her and worked with her.

12.
Curtain Call

"I'm crazy for musicals. We're looking. I'm available."

–Karen Carpenter on Good Morning America, *August 1981*

The vast majority of Karen's friends and associates, when asked what she might be doing today had she lived, insist that she would be devoting her professional life to making music. Posed with the hypothetical question, most showbiz veterans, journalists and disk jockeys provide a variation on that theme. Wrecking Crew drummer Hal Blaine, who played on many Carpenters records, is one of just a few exceptions. He's convinced that most of her time would be spent doing something else. From the time she started performing professionally, it was obvious how much Karen adored children, and Blaine reasons that based on that fondness she would have started a school of some sort.

That's a fair assumption—a school, a youth arts foundation, a musically-oriented charitable group for youngsters, even a research and educational organization devoted to helping young people with the same afflictions from which she suffered. It is also quite fair to assume that making music would never be completely absent from her life, though with the popular music business being what it is today, Karen's role in it would be very distinct and highly selective.

Perhaps she would have created a series of high-profile duets, similar to what Tony Bennett has done with a number of artists over the last few years (many of which were produced by her solo album producer, Phil Ramone), or an entire collection of Great American Songbook classics. Several artists from her era did that in the early 2000s, among them Carly Simon, whose *Moonlight Serenade* album featured songs by Cole Porter, Richard Rodgers, Lorenz Hart, and Glenn Miller, and Rod Stewart, whose *It Had to Be You: The Great American Songbook* featured standards by George & Ira Gershwin. Karen's few contributions to the genre were well done, such as "When I Fall in Love," by Victor Young and Edward Heyman, and a popular medley she sang with Ella Fitzgerald for the 1980 television special *Music, Music, Music*. That medley, which was made available on one of the later compilation CDs, includes portions of "Someone to Watch Over Me" by the Gershwins, "Don't Get Around Much Anymore" by Duke Ellington and Bob Russell, and several others. Karen was well-suited to the style.

A lot can happen in thirty years. Popular singers are not immune from that inevitability, and certainly Karen would not have been, either. Many artists from the 1970s, such as Helen Reddy, Anne Murray, Toni Tennille, Olivia Newton-John, and Petula Clark, are no longer recording or performing today to any perceptible degree. Each has had significant personal challenges, simply fell out of love with the spotlight, or just got tired.

Helen Reddy took to the stage when the hits subsided, appearing in such productions as *Anything Goes, Call Me Madam*, and *The Mystery of Edwin Drood*. She was diagnosed with Addison's disease in 1976 and retired from recording and performing activities in 2002. She is now a practicing clinical hypnotherapist and motivational speaker.

Anne Murray decided to stop recording studio albums after 1988 and announced her complete retirement in 2009. She then founded a nonprofit association in Nova Scotia to help find employment for people who lost their jobs when all the local coal mines closed, and has her own charity golf classic in support of colon cancer research.

Olivia Newton-John battled breast cancer in 1992, co-developed the Olivia Newton-John Cancer and Wellness Centre with Austin Health in Melbourne, Australia, helped develop a product called Liv Aid for breast self-exams, and scaled back her musical activity significantly.

Toni Tennille, who is now separated from the Captain (Daryl Dragon), spent much of the 1980s singing with big bands and symphony orchestras to satisfy a creative urge that passed her by during her pop music days. Then, once the century ended, she began to relegate musical activities to special events and benefits. A dog lover, for the last few years Tennille has been competing her Australian Shepherd dogs at shows, and she is also a registered therapy dog owner who regularly visits patients at hospitals.

Petula Clark stayed musically vibrant for many years following the heyday of her recording career, but in the theatre more than the recording studio. She played Norma Desmond in *Sunset Boulevard* in London from 1995 through 1997, and in the U.S. in 1998. In 2000, she performed a one-woman theatrical show that was essentially a musical autobiography.

Like them, Karen probably would have done theater, maybe even to the present day, and perhaps movies, as well. She was arguably more natural and at ease at musical-comedy bits during television appearances than she was simply introducing songs, chatting with costars, or being interviewed. Plus, she displayed an aptitude for stage direction and movement. She was also a very good mimic, often making friends laugh with her personality parodies. That speaks to a theatricality she rarely had a chance to exhibit for the first few years as part of the Carpenters.

She said several times, in fact, that theater was something she wanted to explore. Deejay Charlie Tuna says that she mentioned to him on a number of occasions during their annual on-air interviews that the musical-comedy stage was never far from her mind. Doug Haverty, who worked with the Carpenters at A&M Records and chatted often with Karen, heard the same thing from her on numerous occasions.

"Besides music, Karen and I both shared an interest in live theater and also in anything having to do with Disney," Haverty recalls. "She admitted to me that she'd love to do a Broadway show. In fact, that was on her list of goals. I believe there was an actress in her, and with the right director she would have simply astounded us on stage. We would have been astonished by the engaging, rich tapestry of honest emotion, and humor, she would have revealed. It wouldn't be entirely dissimilar from the effect she had on fans whenever she would bare her soul in the plaintive ballads she sang so beautifully."

In an episode of ABC's *Good Morning America*, Karen, despite her exceedingly gaunt appearance, seemed hopeful about her future—a future that she imagined would be divided between working with Richard as part of the Carpenters, and working alone. "I would like to do a movie," she told host Joan Lunden. "I would like to do a musical. I've always wanted to do that. I'm crazy for musicals. We're looking. I'm available."

In addition to being a source of fun for her, theater and film might also have been a way for her to be in a creative spotlight without discounting Richard's bearing on her career. He had stated that musical theater was something in which he had little interest, and he almost certainly had no desire to act.

Several of Karen's musical contemporaries had become involved with motion pictures at similar stages in their careers, mostly, but not always, in musically-oriented projects. Helen Reddy had the part of a singing nun in 1974's *Airport '75*; in 1978, Olivia Newton-John starred with John Travolta in *Grease*; Bette Midler played a Janice Joplin-like character in *The Rose* in 1979; and Linda Ronstadt, who appeared on stage in *The Pirates of Penzance* from 1980 to 1982, appeared in the 1983 film version. Karen could very well have, and probably would have loved to, join this special club in the early 1980s, had she sought such opportunities before it was too late.

13.
When Time Was All He Had

"I feel very grateful to be able to make my living doing something I love."
–Richard Carpenter, in the PBS documentary Close to You: Remembering the Carpenters

When compared to the Carpenters' heyday, Richard has clearly been relatively free of the limelight since Karen died. From almost all accounts and the comments from those who follow his career, it seems for him to simply be a case of knowing that a musical livelihood alone or with someone else would never have been as special as it was with Karen.

In many ways, his steadiest job over the last thirty-two years has been to protect and promote the Carpenters' legacy. He has done an enormous amount on that front, both for domestic and foreign markets. It has kept him very busy.

Still, a curious observer might ask, given the enormous depth of his producing, arranging, and performing skills, why he didn't make much of an effort to build an entirely new and distinct career in the years following the end of the Carpenters era.

Certainly he hasn't been absent from the scene entirely. He has been married since 1984, has five children, and is an active and respected patron of the arts in his home region. He sporadically performs both domestically and abroad, and sometimes works with other artists. He also philanthropically helps support the Richard & Karen Carpenter Performing Arts Center at California

State University, Long Beach (which has a Carpenters exhibit), and he and his wife Mary created the Carpenter Family Foundation to help fund several initiatives in healthcare and the arts. One of its programs was the renovation of a theater at Westlake High School in Thousand Oaks, CA, which is now called the Carpenter Family Theatre.

Two years after losing Karen, he found the strength to begin planning for and recording an album of his own, called *Time*, which was released in the summer of 1987. Richard sings several songs and shares the spotlight with such guest vocalists as Dusty Springfield and Dionne Warwick. One of the songs he composed and sings on the album is called "When Time Was All We Had," a tribute to Karen, with lyrics by Pamela Phillips-Oland, whose songs have been recorded by Frank Sinatra, Aretha Franklin, Peabo Bryson, Whitney Houston, Selena, and dozens of other artists. On a website associated with Carnegie Hall, Phillips-Oland reported that she wrote several Christmas songs with Richard for a planned new holiday CD.

Twelve years after *Time*, Richard came out with another album, *Richard Carpenter: Pianist, Arranger, Composer, Conductor*, in which he presents luxuriant piano versions of several tunes originally recorded by the Carpenters.

For Japan's Akiko Kobayashi, whose voice has been compared to Karen's, Richard produced and arranged a 1988 album called *City of Angels*. For Claire de la Fuente, a Filipino singer who has often been called the Karen Carpenter of the Philippines, he worked on a 2008 album called *Something in Your Eyes*, whose title song he also wrote.

These projects and others have not given Richard even a fraction of the public recognition he used to enjoy. One might wonder if the kind of post-Karen career he has had was simply predestined, or if he in some way engineered it that way—and if so, for what reason. Those who don't mind swimming in potentially murky waters might ask just how much such gremlins as guilt or regret have to do with it.

Harry Sharpe, a music director who worked with Richard at the Hollywood Bowl, agrees with those who say that Richard doubted that anyone else could inspire him to write and arrange music the way Karen did. The few post-Karen projects Richard tried left him discontented. "I heard that he never found anyone that he particularly wanted to work with. He tried several projects with other artists, and a couple of those ended without being completed because of personality conflicts," says Sharpe, who worked with Donna Summer when she and the Carpenters were being inducted into the Hollywood Bowl Hall of Fame. "Everyone agrees that what Karen and Richard had was unique and could never be duplicated. At some level, I'm sure Richard knew that, and never desired to even try."

The Carpenters, who first performed at the Hollywood Bowl in 1966 at a "Battle of the Bands" event, were inducted into its Hall of Fame in 2010, with Summer and French pianist Jean-Yves Thibaudet. Herb Alpert made the presentation to Richard, who had returned to the venue for the first time since the group played to sold-out crowds there during their heyday. At the ceremony, Richard conducted the Hollywood Bowl Orchestra in a medley of Carpenters hits, and then, playing a grand piano, accompanied a video of Karen singing "For All We Know." Following his acceptance speech, he once more accompanied a video of Karen, this time singing "We've Only Just Begun." Richard also performed the song "Iced Tea," which he had composed for the Richard Carpenter Trio, and which was one of the tunes the group played when they won the Battle of the Bands contest. Forty-four years after first appearing at the iconic concert hall, Richard, in a way, had come full circle—though it is a milestone that merely adds to the complexity of assessing his post-Carpenters career.

Part of the reason it is so difficult to assess is because Richard seems to want to micromanage and mitigate all activities related to the Carpenters' history and heritage. Plus, he's given relatively few interviews which, intentionally or not, leaves the notion that he'd prefer for the heritage to remain exactly the way it is, no matter how incomplete or watered down. He's talked sporadi-cally to reporters and interviewers at magazines and on radio and television shows, but rarely shared more than what was already known. In October 2014, he told radio host Chris May that he has decided to give no more interviews at all.

Just how he really feels deep down about what happened to Karen, his role, what could have been, and what has transpired in the intervening years, might never be known.

What *is* known—though not to the extent he deserves—is the durability and sophistication of the music he wrote and arranged. Most of the melodies Richard composed are memorable, and his arrangements are multi-textured tapestries that have been stud-ied at such prestigious institutions as the Berklee College of Mu-sic in Boston and Stanford University in California.

Like the best movie scores, Richard's orchestrations add color and dimension to songs without throwing a bright spotlight on just what it was he did to achieve the effect. One of the earliest hits, "For All We Know," fits that bill, with the strength of brass support acting as nothing more than a cushion that works to the song's advantage. A discussion of his arrangement for "Let Me Be the One" appears in a serious music journal, based solely on his counterintuitive placement of an off-beat brass burst in the chorus. Noted musicologist Daniel Levitan (who is also a cognitive psychologist and neuroscientist) has assessed Richard's skill many times in industry publications. "He gives each instrument a unique place," he once wrote in *Electronic Musician*. "Featured instruments weave in and out of the spotlight filling holes where necessary, but never stepping on each other." He has also discussed how Richard uses instrumentation to compliment Karen's voice, and other engaging tricks of the trade.

As both an arranger and pianist, Richard revealed a solid grip on blues and jazz in such recordings as "This Masquerade" and "A Song for You" (both composed by Leon Russell). He demonstrated his proficiency on the keyboards in such numbers as "Dizzy Fingers" and "Flat Baroque." "Dizzy Fingers" was performed for the 1980 Carpenters TV special *Music, Music, Music,* in a bit that had Richard running from one type of keyboard to another, including an upright, a grand, a harpsichord, and a toy piano.

"It's sad to say, but there hasn't been nearly enough ink about Richard's prowess, his skills, his gift as a producer and arranger," commented John Bettis on Chris May's radio interview show. He spoke of how Richard arranged every note on most of the Carpenters' records, and how he was able to hear songs in their entirety, in his head, even before they were finished being arranged and recorded. Richard, Bettis said, could hear thirteen separate musical effects simultaneously, including notes, harmonies, and background rhythms.

Richard was also highly adept at recognizing a song's potential for the Carpenters to record just from hearing a few bars on the radio, in a movie, at a club, from a commercial, or by reading them on a lead sheet. The most famous and oft-quoted example, of course, is when he watched a Crocker Bank commercial on television, took note of the theme song, and soon after had a hit with Paul Williams' and Roger Nichols' "We've Only Just Begun." Several Carpenters songs came from albums recorded by other groups first and given a brand new and often fuller life under Richard's guidance. One of the first recordings of "Hurting Each Other" was by Chad Allan and the Expressions (which later changed its name to the Guess Who). An obscure band from Connecticut called the Wildweeds recorded an original song called "And When She Smiles" that, in the Carpenters' hands, became the lilting "And When He Smiles." It was included on the 2004 *When Time Goes By* compilation. A few Carpenters songs came from movies. Others were handed to Richard by songwriters and publishers.

Like any gifted composer and arranger, Richard needed a talented band to carry out his musical vision. He would accept nothing less than precision. Toward that end, he also had the knack to gauge talent wherever he saw it. Several instrumentalists came and went through the years for both recording in the studio and going out on tour, but several stayed for most or all of the entire run of the band. What is significant is that many of them, while enormously skilled, were still very young and relatively new to professional recording and international touring, yet Richard knew they'd be exceptional in their assigned musical tasks. He knew that even despite the fact that they were not all cut from the same cloth; the band members were rather dissimilar, what with Doug Strawn (reeds, keyboards, vocals) being known as vivacious, Bob Messenger (sax, flute) as restrained, and the others—guitarists Gary Sims and Tony Peluso and bass guitarist Danny Woodhams—as having various other personality traits. (Richard had worked with many of them during the Spectrum days.)

Richard wanted the band to recreate on stage the exact sounds that record buyers heard at home, and the band members were both talented enough as musicians and dedicated enough to Richard to do just that—even though it can be hard for musicians to restrain themselves in concert from taking a few musical flights of fancy. Most concert performers thrive on that; the Carpenters avoided it.

Based solely on his undeniable talent, it is likely that Richard would have had a busy career in music even if there hadn't been a Karen (or if she had decided not to join him)—probably not as an internationally famous recording star, however. As a potential front man for a pop group he may not have been endearing enough for the 1970's public. A lisp notwithstanding, Richard had a fine singing voice—strong, sturdy, and precise—but his magnetism (what is sometimes called the Q score) was likely not strong enough for the court of collective approval.

Despite her deep-rooted personal issues, Karen was in many ways the normal one, at least in public; Richard was the impenetrable and awkward maestro. Karen, for all her problems, helped balance her brother's awkwardness with the sweetness of her own, simple, unaffected, girl-next-door appeal.

In the PBS documentary *Close to You: Remembering the Carpenters*, Richard stated that he was very grateful to be able to make his living doing something he loved. "But what makes it that much better," he added, "is that my sister happened to be one of the finest female singers who ever lived, and enjoyed making records as much as I enjoyed making them."

Richard was blessed to have his sister as a muse with her matchless voice and public charm, and Karen benefited enormously from her brother's musical insights and unwavering efforts. Success may have been destined, but Richard and Karen required each other's gifts in order for that destiny to be fulfilled.

14.
Music, Music, Music

"Richard and I believe that there's enough people around to have all kinds of music. There's enough room for everybody."

–Karen Carpenter, on FM100, Los Angeles, 1978

Ask enough people to name different types of music and some-where down the line, along with rock, jazz, classical, country, and others, someone is likely to say "Carpenters music." But once you take the Carpenters' entire recorded catalog into serious consider-ation (which many non-fans will never be willing to do), it becomes evident that a one-size-fits-all category just won't do the trick.

Within their many albums, including some compiled after Karen's death taken both from studio and television show recording sessions, can be found everything from smoky renditions of power ballads like "This Masquerade" and "A Song for You," to offbeat novelties like "Goofus" and "Calling Occupants of Interplanetary Craft." They recorded a number of Great American Songbook classics, such as "Little Girl Blue" by Richard Rodgers and Lorenz Hart, and "I Can Dream, Can't I?" by Sammy Fein and Irving Kahal. Golden oldies pop up here and there, including a sixties medley that features "The End of the World" and "Johnny Angel," among others. Songs with Cajun and calypso roots, such as "Jambalaya (On the Bayou)" and "Man Smart, Woman Smarter," respectively, are intriguing counterpoints to re-imagined tunes first recorded by the Beatles, such as "Help" and "Ticket to Ride," and Neil Sedaka, such as "Breaking Up is Hard to Do" and "Solitaire."

Several country-flavored tunes are in the mix, including "Reason to Believe" and "Sweet, Sweet Smile," as are songs from motion picture soundtracks, such as "For All We Know" from 1970's *Lovers and Other Strangers*, "Bless the Beasts and the Children" from the 1971 movie of the same name, and "Ordinary Fool," written by Paul Williams for 1976's *Bugsy Malone*.

There are far more Christmas songs than the three or four that most radio stations seem to play again and again during the holidays. In fact, they recorded so many Christmas songs for 1978's *Christmas Portrait* that Richard had more than enough for 1984's *An Old-Fashioned Christmas* (the year after Karen died).

There are also many other compositions by distinguished songwriters and songwriting teams, including, of course, Richard Carpenter and John Bettis. Roger Nichols, who co-wrote several Carpenters hits with Paul Williams, also teamed with Dean Pitchford, who wrote the screenplay for *Footloose* and collaborated on its score, to provide a solemn and idyllic love elegy called "Now," recorded in April 1982. It told the story of a woman at peace with her life because of a special love that gives her all the confidence she needs to face the future. It was a swan song that the swan never got to hear in its finished form:

"Now when I wake there's someone home
I'll never face the nights alone
You gave me courage I need to win
To open my heart and to let you in
And I never really knew how, until now, until now."

It was the last song Karen recorded.

It is the range of musical and thematic styles that should disallow the Carpenters' recorded catalog from being relegated to a single label—such as 'the Carpenters sound' to which many people have referred in the past. At one point on the spectrum, for example, there is "Sometimes," which features Karen's single voice and a lone piano, but at another there's "Without a Song," which uses dozens of voices, all provided by Karen and Richard, with orchestral strings and horns toward the end. For every up-tempo, affirmative love song like "Top of the World," there are others of chilly desolation, such as "At the End of a Song," which claims that there is nowhere on earth where life is not crazy or hearts not distressed. Even their many love-is-blue songs differ considerably from one another in mood and cadence: "(I'm Caught Between) Goodbye and I Love You" has Karen diving into one of her deepest registers with a melancholy that is nonetheless tranquil, while "All You Get From Love is a Love Song" has an almost bouncy, danceable beat with which Karen reaches higher on the scale to sing about the inevitability of unrequited love.

The lyrics to many of the sad songs (happy ones, too) were written by John Bettis, who knew Karen as well as anyone in their entourage. He once commented that he and Karen were so emotionally alike that he could write about her and write about himself and have it always be the same tone of voice. One can only hope that Bettis was being more poetic than pragmatic in some of his more melodramatic moments as a lyricist.

The Carpenters' first three hits *were* basically good-spirited stories of optimistic love, "(They Long to Be) Close To You," "We've Only Just Begun," and "For All We Know," and there were many others later on. However, once Karen's story comes center stage, the focus invariably goes to all the songs she sang about sorrow, loneliness, despair, and longing. There are many of them, and she sings them with unsettling intimacy. That's why it is refreshing to hear Karen sing a song like "Leave Yesterday Behind" with equal conviction:

"When the morning sunrise
Becomes a magic show
Before your very eyes

And all the sounds of life
Begin to harmonize.

You hear a song of hope
Surround your senses
And feel the promise of
A brand new kind of world.

Unwind and follow me
Come let me help you see
How to find a way
To leave yesterday behind."

"Leave Yesterday Behind," however, did not appear on an album until 2004's As Time Goes By compilation, more than two decades after Karen passed away.

Karen sang other uplifting tunes with the same kind of sincerity, most of which were shared publicly during her lifetime. These included "Those Good Old Dreams," an acknowledgement of wishes coming true, "Sing," about the pleasure of music, and "Top of the World." In fact, all three were released as singles, with "Top of the World" reaching #1 on the charts in 1973, and "Sing" reaching #3 the same year. Only "Those Good Old Dreams" failed to catch on in the same way, topping out at #63 in 1981, once the gold had already faded.

Despite the broad diversity of their catalog, the references to a Carpenters sound may never cease. Naturally, Karen's voice alone can be responsible for that impression, but if that's the case, then the number of groups and performers who have their own exclusive 'sound' would be incalculable. That's rarely considered a negative. Although Richard and Karen were proud of their work, they understood the inevitability of insolent comments and opinions and found themselves both defending and explaining their music from time to time.

Interviewed on radio in 1978, Karen speculated that with harder rock being prevalent in the record stores and on the airwaves at the time they were coming up, the Carpenters' style of music may have caught many radio listeners by surprise, yet it was still interesting enough to avoid instantly turning them off. She further proposed that quite a number of people were actually waiting for something like their sound to arrive on the airwaves and in the record stores. "Richard and I still believe that there's enough people around to have all kinds of music. It doesn't have to be one kind. There's enough room for everybody."

"It's not a sound that ever really was that trendy," Richard told Joan Lunden in a 1981 interview on ABC's *Good Morning America*. "Things will come and go, and the kind of music we do will always be there."

In some cases, albums are more than just a collection of songs; they can also be time capsules that store many of the emotions and conflicts that were part of the artists' lives at the time each album was being made. If that's true, then several Carpenters albums can be used to help tell the story of Richard and Karen Carpenter.

Richard and Karen had plenty of emotions and conflicts that seriously affected at least half of their studio albums, but they also had enormous strengths that disallowed any of those albums from being regarded as complete failures. At least that's the way two factions viewed it: their fans, and to an extent, A&M.

Fans always found (and continue to find) plenty to enjoy, to admire, to comfort them. For no matter what kind of genre a Carpenters song happens to be, or how that song is orchestrated, there is the constancy of Karen's plaintive voice and the finely-crafted arrangements played by consummate professions to back it up.

As far as A&M was concerned, certainly the executives would have much preferred for the last few albums to have burned up the charts and earn more money than they did. They knew, however, that the Carpenters always provided a little more than mere bread and butter for the distinctive brand. Cofounder

Jerry Moss did express his concern to Richard from time to time about the artistic direction of an album and the sales route that followed. But he also knew that the group represented and, in all likelihood, would continue to represent at least one of the decisive reasons his company was so successful, and why he and Herb Alpert were, in turn, such wealthy men.

Would Alpert and Moss, and Richard and Karen, have been able to build further on their success if the Carpenters had selected a more trendy musical genre? Would there have been even more success if they had changed with the times—or even if they had changed just for the sake of experimentation?

They did want to do a country album at one time, but Moss was against the idea. Karen enjoyed country music and, when appropriate, adopted a county style of singing; she was, in fact, the one who suggested they record Juice Newton's "Sweet, Sweet Smile," which Karen had heard on an advanced copy of a Newton album. The single subsequently became the first Carpenters song to place on the American Country music charts. A number of pop artists who crossed over to country found success, and the Carpenters might possibly have been one of them had they pursued the notion.

If Richard had decided to back away from his aversion to disco, which was extremely popular toward the end of the 1970s, the Carpenters might also have found an intriguing and lucrative new path to take, onto which they could have put their own inimitable stamp. Karen's friend Olivia Newton-John did that in 1981—just as Richard and Karen were putting together their comeback *Made in America* album—with what became the best-selling single of the 1980s, "Physical." Newton-John won a Grammy for Best Female Pop Vocal Performance for that record.

Karen would have put a committed effort behind whatever new style she and her brother selected, simply because she loved just about all of them. Through the years, she mentioned how much she enjoyed everyone from Barbra Streisand to Donna Summer, and many others in between.

Even had they gone out on a musical limb, it may not have mattered much by the 1980s simply because the lines in the sand had already formed separating those who loved the Carpenters unconditionally from those who couldn't tolerate them no matter what. What's more, sometimes there were highly-respected individuals who readily dismissed the group, and others who adored them who themselves were not necessarily well liked. Robert Christgau, often called the dean of American rock critics, called Karen's voice a "dispassionate contralto" and did not seem to put much weight behind the group's significance, referring to their success as "statistical" more than anything else; meanwhile, after a visit by the Carpenters to the White House, Richard Nixon publicly called them "Young America at its very best." In essence, an overall assessment of their reputation was always somewhat difficult to judge.

Is it the music that groups or performers leave behind that defines their legacy, or is it the music in conjunction with the story of their lives? Maybe it's both.

In the 1970s, the Carpenters' success depended to a great extent on their albums. Their live shows broke no new ground, and they didn't find their TV niche until late in the game. For better or worse, their albums, briefly described below, are a time capsule of their noteworthy yet unsettled personal and professional lives.

Offering (1969) later had its name changed to *Ticket to Ride* after the Carpenters started to become popular. A ballad version of the Beatles' "Ticket to Ride" was the sole single off this first A&M album. Some of the songs on *Offering* had been Spectrum standards from two years earlier (several written by Richard Carpenter and John Bettis, or by Richard alone) and originally recorded in Joe Osborn's garage studio. The album's eventual name change was one of two elements to be revisited for future albums: the other was that where Richard sang lead on several songs on this first album, he stopped doing so as they moved forward, except in a few cases. Also, Karen played bass guitar on two songs; she had learned how to play from Joe Osborn.

Close to You (1970) is the album many consider to be the Carpenters' true debut simply because it featured their first two hit singles, "(They Long to Be) Close to You" and "We've Only Just Begun." In addition, it has ten other pleasant if not necessarily remarkable tunes that benefit from Richard's arrangements and Karen's vocals. These include the Beatles' "Help," Burt Bacharach and Hal David's "I'll Never Fall in Love Again," and four compositions by Richard Carpenter and John Bettis: "Maybe It's You," which combines a conventional love ballad with an almost spiritual aura; "Crescent Noon," a shadowy tale of time that showcases Karen's richest and deepest register; "Mr. Guder," which was Richard and John's firebrand attempt to insult the boss who had fired them from their jobs at Disneyland; and "Another Song," a four-and-a-half minute cut, more than half of which is an instrumental that starts out in a Baroque style and ends up more as avant-garde jazz. *Close to You* was listed as #175 on *Rolling Stone's* 2003 list of the "500 Greatest Albums of All Time." The magazine wrote, "With their lush music and thoroughly wholesome image, Richard and Karen Carpenter epitomized the early Seventies mainstream. Years later, as soft rock became a hipster touchstone, the chaste elegance of ballads like 'Close to You' and 'We've Only Just Begun' influenced many cooler, scruffier indie bands."

Carpenters (1971), often referred to as 'the Tan Album,' had three songs that made it onto the Top 10 singles chart, "Rainy Days and Mondays," "Superstar," and "For All We Know." Also featured is "Hideaway," written by Randy Sparks, the founder of the New Christy Minstrels, who also owned the Los Angeles club Ledbetters, where Richard first heard him perform the song on a night when Spectrum was performing there. It's another one of those sad numbers that in retrospect are sadly biographical for Karen ("I'd like to find a place to hide away, far from the shadows of my mind . . . .") Another song on *Carpenters* is "One Love," which Richard Carpenter and John Bettis wrote to acknowledge their infatuation with a pretty waitress at Disneyland. At less than two-and-a-half minutes, "Let Me Be the One," by Paul Williams and Roger Nichols, is one of their shortest cuts, but has a hook that lasts long after the song is over. The album won a Grammy Award for Outstanding Performance by a Duo, Group or Chorus.

A Song for You (1972) is named for the Leon Russell tune that leads off (and ends) the album—a song that *Rolling Stone* magazine called the project's finest moment. (Russell also wrote "Superstar" from the previous album, with Bonnie Bramlett.) In addition to Karen's sultry vocal, "A Song for You" features a strong tenor sax solo played by band member Bob Messenger. Top 20 hits from the disc include "Hurting Each Other," "It's Going to Take Some Time," "Goodbye to Love," and "I Won't Last a Day Without You." ("Top of the World," another hit, is also on the album but had been released several months before the LP came out.) The story is often told of how many fans were outraged, and how many new ones were won over, by the gruff fuzz guitar solo Richard decided to add to "Goodbye to Love," played by Tony Peluso. Richard names *A Song for You* as the best Carpenters album and has stated that what he likes, among other things, are many of the creative production elements, such as the bookended use of the title track at the beginning and end.

Now & Then (1973) represented a bit of a change in format in that one side represents "now" and the other "then," with a medley of oldies. Richard said that he was aware that many radio stations were starting to change to an oldies format at the time, which is what prompted his decision. The medley included, among others, "The End of the World," "Johnny Angel," "Dead Man's Curve," "The Night Has a Thousand Eyes," and "One Fine Day." (Richard sings lead on three of them.) "One Fine Day" is the second Carole King melody that the Carpenters recorded, the first being "It's Going to Take Some Time" from the previous album. "Yesterday Once More," composed by Richard with lyrics by John Bettis, was another nod to the direction radio playlists were taking— and turned into one of the Carpenters' biggest worldwide hits. "Sing" was another big hit from the album and the Carpenters' seventh gold single. Arguably the most sophisticated entry is "This

Masquerade," which was also composed by Leon Russell. It is highlighted by Karen's bluesy maturity (she was twenty-three but sounded as if she had been singing in smoky nightclubs for twenty years) and also by its two solos, one by Richard on piano and the other by Bob Messenger on flute. Although the "now" and "then" concept stood well enough on its own, it has also been suggested that Richard eagerly went for it because he lacked the time he needed to listen to as many demo songs as he had in the past.

Also in 1973, after the Carpenters' first five albums, A&M released *The Singles: 1969-1973*, which featured a dozen of their radio hits.

Horizon (1975) had the distinction of including another top seller not just in the U.S., but internationally, "Please Mr. Postman." The song was a hit for the Marvelettes in 1961 and was covered by the Beatles the following year for their second LP. "Only Yesterday" was the album's other big hit. Even though it was one of their shortest albums, *Rolling Stone* called *Horizon* one of the Carpenters' most musically sophisticated efforts, and that's partially due to the fact that it benefited from the technical sophistication that came with the studio's new 24-track recording process. (Previously A&M artists worked with 16-track equipment.) "Solitaire," written by Neil Sedaka and Phil Cody, seems to be an excuse to show off Karen's low register rather than to offer any sort of musical elegance (Karen stated that she didn't like it very much), and the Eagles' "Desperado" doesn't generate too much excitement, either. Furthering the 'yesterday' theme, the album features the 1938 Fein/Kahal song, "I Can Dream, Can't I?" Richard brought in noted musical veteran Billy May to arrange it in an authentic 1940's style.

A Kind of Hush (1976) has the unfortunate distinction of being the project that coincided with the darkest days of Richard's Quaalude addiction. He, and others, have called the album bland, and he blamed its blandness on poor song selection, which in turn can be traced to his personal problems. It was regarded as somewhat lackluster and too similar to what the Carpenters had already done. "Sandy" is a pleasant though rather conventional and chaste love song composed by Richard and lyricist John Bettis. "Happy" sounds more uninspired than happy. The past returns once more with the title song, the nine-year-old Herman's Hermits hit "A Kind of Hush," and the 1962 Neil Sedaka/Howard Greenfield standard, "Breaking Up Is Hard to Do" (which Sedaka himself remade the previous year as a ballad). Saving the album from oblivion is the lush and sanguine ballad "One More Time" (it, too, is about running away) and "I Need to Be in Love," Karen's favorite Carpenters song of all time, and a production of significant command and emotion.

Passage (1977) has been called innovative and surprising, as well as daring and satisfying, having such unique selections as "Don't Cry for Me, Argentina" from the musical *Evita*, and "Calling Occupants of Interplanetary Craft (The Recognized Anthem of World Contact Day)." Richard initially considered "Don't Cry for Me, Argentina" a perfect match for Karen's strengths, but later thought otherwise. Curiously, there are no songs written by Richard Carpenter and John Bettis on *Passage*. "I Just Fall in Love Again," at four minutes, was deemed too long for an AM radio single release. (It became a hit single for Anne Murray in 1979—in a two minute, fifty-two second version.) While Richard had asked others to help with orchestrations occasionally in the past, this time he had three songs orchestrated by Peter Knight. *Passage* was the first Carpenters album not to reach Gold status (500,000 units sold).

Christmas Portrait (1978) has seventeen holiday classics (thirty, if you count the individual songs included in its few medleys), which prompted Richard to comment that this was the album that tested the limitations and capabilities of a single piece of long-playing vinyl. The album sold more than 2 million copies. The support of Carpenters fans was at least one of the contributing factors to its healthy sales, along with the fact that a large segment of the population simply loves Christmas albums. Plus, the infectious enthusiasm Richard and Karen had for making the album in the first place piqued interest even before it went on sale.

Made in America (1981) came after a two-and-a-half year hiatus from any original recording at all. For Richard, who had turned over many of the Christmas album's details to others and had taken a year off from the music business entirely, it had really been four years since he worked on a conventional Carpenters album. As far as Karen was concerned, she was coming off the New York experience and the California reaction to her solo album project, and had gotten married to a man she knew she'd be unable to stay married to. So it makes perfect sense that Made in America is often is referred to as the Carpenters' comeback album. And its contents make good on the promise, with such solidly produced compositions as "Those Good Old Dreams," "I Believe You," "When It's Gone (It's Just Gone)," "Touch Me When We're Dancing," and "When You've Got What it Takes." There is a certain maturity to Karen's performances on Made in America that was not as predominant on previous efforts. Both Richard and Karen said this was one of their favorite albums.

Voice of the Heart came out several months after Karen passed away. "Now" and "You're Enough" were taken from Karen's final recording session the year before, and the other eight selections were taken from tapes made in previous years, originally intended for other projects and then stored away. These included "At the End of a Song," "Two Lives," "Make Believe It's Your First Time" (recorded for Karen's solo album) and "Ordinary Fool," written by Paul Williams for the 1976 movie "Bugsy Malone," a 1940's gangster spoof starring teenage actors Scott Baio and Jodie Foster. Voice of the Heart has an eclectic mix of tunes, with various styles and moods, but no Top 40 singles came out of it.

In addition to the studio albums produced with Karen's active participation, Richard and A&M compiled several others afterward, including Lovelines in 1989, with eleven songs (including another from her solo project); Interpretations: A 25th Anniversary Celebration in 1994, with sixteen tracks (the anniversary it refers to is the Carpenters' association with A&M, which began in 1969); the four-disk CD *Essential Collection: 1965-1997* in 2002, which in addition to dozens of songs also includes a few outtakes, TV commercials, and several cuts from their pre-A&M days; and *As Time Goes By* in 2004, another large compilation. This one has several medleys, including one Karen did with Perry Como on the 1974 *Perry Como Christmas Show* and another with Ella Fitzgerald from 1980's *The Carpenters: Music, Music, Music* special.

Postscript:
Hanging on a Hope

"The endless crowds of faces, just keep on wearing a smile."

–from the song "Road Ode," *on the album* A Song for You

As this book neared completion, the 33rd anniversary of Karen's death was just a few months away. We know a little more about anorexia nervosa by virtue of the fact that more people identified as anorexic have been treated by more professionals who have researched and documented the causes, effects, and treatments. But even if we knew everything there was to know about Karen Carpenter, we still might not be able to discover and reconstruct all the specific reasons and causes that contributed to her early demise.

Nor can we know how Karen would have fared with different treatment, even if she had lived long enough to try other methods. "We now have years of research, more treatment modalities, and many more treatment facilities; success rates, however, are probably not that much different from several decades ago, which reflects how complicated and multifaceted an illness anorexia is," says Dr. Amy Nulsen. "Despite what we have learned, our culture, to a large degree, still values and reinforces thinness. The patient has to be ready to take on the struggle and do that hard work of letting go by exploring and understanding the meaning behind their symptoms and finding healthy ways of dealing with their troubling issues. It's really hard work, but it can be liberating."

Karen was never truly liberated, and to find out why she got to the point where such liberation was even necessary we would have to go all the way back to her roots in New Haven, Connecticut, follow her around inside and outside the house, and do a comprehensive day-by-day, year-by-year evaluation. But those early days of her life were only meagerly documented. Also, the most important answers are probably based on what went on in her head, not always in the living room or out on the softball field. A complete evaluation is practically impossible.

Richard deserves his privacy. Although it is frustrating to fans (and writers) that he neither supports nor would likely be appreciative of any decisive attempt to fully explore his sister's past, to delve into his and their mother's role in her life, or to help shed any other light, it is his right to hold that view. The television movie he agreed to have produced in 1988, *The Karen Carpenter Story*, which aired the following January, was so patchy and watered down that people who do know many of the biographical details find it almost laughable. (Still, *The Karen Carpenter Story* was the highest-rated two-hour television movie of 1989 and the third-highest-rated TV film on any of the national broadcast networks during the entire decade.) Ever since then, millions have wanted to know more, thousands became determined to look for more, and dozens decided to actively research and publish more.

Adding further speculation that there are stories behind the stories is the fact that Karen's husband, Tom Burris, was allegedly paid by the Carpenter family to refrain, for the rest of his life, from discussing Karen and their marriage. The mere existence of such an accord adds to the sometimes reckless speculation about just what he knew or observed. It is also possible, of course, that the family simply worried about Burris making up sordid tales, for he had already proven himself a fraud and pretender in his relationship with Karen.

Still, the more discoveries made about Karen's life, the eerier it becomes when we focus on many of the lyrics that she sang so compellingly. Is it silly to try make more of the connection than there really is? Perhaps. Then again, trying to analyze why so many people enjoy listening to depressing songs can be equally futile, but no less intriguing:

"Rainy Days and Mondays" . . . "What I've got they used to call the blues. Nothing is really wrong, feeling like I don't belong."

"Goodbye to Love" . . . "No one ever cared if I should live or die. Time and time again the chance for love has passed me by, and all I know of love is how to live without it."

"Only Yesterday" . . . "In my own time nobody knew the pain I was going through, and waiting was all my heart could do."

"(A Place to) Hideaway" . . . "Knowing tomorrow brings only sorry, where can I go to find a place to hide away?"

"Another Song" . . . "Softly, they said, all my favorite dreams were dead, leaving a cloud of sadness in my head."

"Ordinary Fool" . . . "An ordinary fool, that same old story, seems I was born for the part. It's a lesson to be learned in a page I should have turned. I shouldn't cry, but I do."

"At the End of a Song" . . . "They tell me somewhere this life isn't crazy, but I've traveled the world far and wide, and I say they're wrong."

"One More Time" . . . "Well, I'll just close my eyes and everything's all right. Though I'm really far away, I'll make my getaway."

"I Need to Be in Love" . . . "So here I am with pockets full of good intentions, but none of them will comfort me tonight. I'm wide awake at four A.M., without a friend in sight. I'm hanging on a hope, but I'm all right."

Karen may have been hanging on a hope, but she was not all right. Maybe she never was.

Given that the Carpenters first gained popularity in 1970, had their last Top 10 hit in 1975 and their last Top 20 in 1981, it is almost astounding how much has been written about Karen, and how many people over the years have sought—and still seek—information, recordings, videos, photos, memorabilia, and more.

The Carpenters' legacy was dogged by the impression that they were bland, chaste, sterile, goody-goody. They denied it whenever they could. Yet it is difficult not to grin when you consider that for their 1971 hit "Superstar," they changed the original line, "I can hardly wait to sleep with you again," to "I can hardly wait to *be* with you again," as if to avoid any sexual innuendo. Karen's solo album was designed to have a more ripened aura. Still, for her version of Paul Simon's "Still Crazy After All These Years," Karen asked Simon to replace the lyric, "Four in the morning, crapped out, yawning," to something less egregious, and so it was changed to "Four in the morning, *crashed* out, yawning." Lyric changes like these are tiny points, indeed, but sometimes they leave questions almost as large as the legacy itself.

Such tidbits shouldn't make much of a difference in the overall estimation of any musical career, but somehow with Richard and Karen, they do—without taking anything away from their appeal or an appreciation of their talent. To be sure, in some ways they were, simply, odd, but that, too, is what may have made them unique. In the highly competitive world of entertainment, that can be an important distinction.

As for Karen herself, she was as inscrutable as she was talented, as complex as she was engaging, making her one of the most successful enigmas of the 1970s. She often stated how music was her life and how she loved what she and her brother and their band were able to accomplish. Yet touring was a source of much of her discomfort. From the age of sixteen, when she was signed by Magic Lamp records, to her last recording session in the spring of 1982, she was a working girl who had a hunger for fun, games and friendships, but rarely the time for it. She craved love and a family of her own, even though the list of requisites for a husband narrowed her chances considerably. She was a woman-child who revered Disney animals as much as gold records.

Guitarists Danny Woodhams and Gary Sims, both of whom were in the Carpenters, wrote a song called "Road Ode" that was included on the 1972 album, *A Song For You*. Whether or not they wrote it about themselves or to reflect Karen's own feelings is not clear, but it *was* Karen's voice that convincingly lamented about an inability to find inner peace while pursuing success. Fans back then heard it only as a haunting ballad driven by Karen's low register, *not* necessarily as a hint of the misery and gloom that deeply plagued her:

"The endless crowds of faces
Just keep on wearing a smile
The countless times and places
Lead me back, please take me back home.

I wonder if these feelings ever change
How many times I'll lift this load
Come tomorrow I'll be gone again
Roads of sorrows coming to an end for me."

She and Richard also recorded a song called "Sometimes," a love poem of thanks and appreciation from the narrator to her family, providing quite a contrast to "Road Ode." It was penned as a Christmas present by Felice Mancini, daughter of famed composer and conductor Henry Mancini, to give to her own parents. Henry set it to music. "I often hear from people who play 'Sometimes' and then realize it has a lot of meaning in their lives. I appreciate that and feel great about it," Felice Mancini says. "The sentiment of the song—that we don't say 'thank you' and 'I love you' enough times to the people we care about—seems to resonate with people in a simple and honest way." For Karen, that kind of raw sentiment takes on an almost paradoxical significance as one who struggled for her mother's hard-won affection and may have mutely been seeking her brother's understanding of her innermost needs.

Then, there was her sex appeal. On one hand, disc jockeys on the air were sometimes heard indelicately joking that they'd love to 'nail' Karen Carpenter, who could be filmed and photographed looking quite fetching. On the other hand, there were all those promotional photos and videos that positioned her as a nearly-inseparable white-laced double of her straight-laced brother. Plus, the fact that her looks seemed to vary often—from a little to a lot, for one reason or another—made it difficult for the public to decide exactly where she fit in on the glamour scale.

The perception, for several reasons, is that other than the transparent attempt from her solo album, there was hardly a reference in the Carpenters' song catalog to lovemaking or to any kind of sexuality at all. That, of course, is not entirely true. One notable exception was "I Believe You," which was released as a single in 1978 but didn't appear on an album until *Made in America* in 1981. The song was written by brothers Dick and Don Addrisi, who also wrote "Never My Love," a hit for the Association which was covered by many other artists and for many years was one of the most-played songs on radio and television. In addition to its overt sensuality, "I Believe You" contains an unintended element of sorrow in that it speaks of the child Karen always wanted but never had:

"I believe you
When you say that every time that we make love
Will be the first time we've made love
And every act of love will please you
Baby, I believe you.

I believe you
When you say you'll fill my body with your soul
And love will grow into a freckled little girl
Who looks like we do
Baby, I believe you."

Karen had a lot with which to deal—more than just the issues discussed in all the books and articles and online discussions, which by now number in the tens of thousands. Some of those issues can get quite contentious, such as her sexual orientation, a topic that has consistently churned in the rumor mill. Some people who raise it round up all the usual and entirely clichéd suspects to make their case, such as Karen's low voice, tomboy childhood, and deficient mother-daughter relationship.

Would Karen's legacy have been any different if the Carpenters continued to record together for another decade or two? How would it have been different if Richard or Karen had pursued solo projects that actually made a mark in the marketplace? These are questions for which we can never have good enough answers. Nor, for that matter, will we ever know for sure if the legacy today would have been different than it is had they been marketed in another manner, or if one or the other had been successful in love and romance earlier on.

In the world of entertainment, eventual failure is sometimes blamed on success that comes too early, but artists and entertainers can hardly be blamed for being talented enough to succeed early, and for eagerly accepting that fate. The real question is: can the entertainment industry do a disservice to some artists by lauding them as if they've already proven everything they need to prove, long before they are finished proving it? Might that create too much pressure and raise unreasonable expectations?

Richard himself seemed to question it and understand the irony all too well when host Ralph Edwards surprised him and Karen with a 1971 appearance on *This Is Your Life*. This was a prominent weekly television program in which friends, relatives, and associates surprise unsuspecting famous guests and share all kinds of relevant (and sometimes not so relevant) stories and anecdotes about their lives and careers. The series, which had returned to the air ten years after being a popular mainstay from 1952 to 1961, typically honors performers and others in the public eye after many years and, more often, many decades of plying their trades and making their marks. In the 1971 season, surprised guests included sixty-nine-year-old Irene Ryan (Granny from *The Beverly Hillbillies*), sixty-three-year-old Bette Davis, sixty-three-year-old Ethel

Merman, and fifty-eight-year-old Mary Martin. Even one of the youngest guests that year, thirty-seven-year-old Pat Boone, was still sixteen years older than Karen, who was twenty-one when she was on it. When Edwards' ruse was revealed, it prompted Richard to state, plainly and somewhat alarmed, "We're too young!" He was entirely correct.

Through it all, Karen was always enormously popular and to this day remains deeply missed as a singer and musical treasure. Her lower register was potent; she had an unusual and interesting blend of a New England inflection (with a purposeful hint of some of British crooner Matt Monro's pronunciation—especially with words like "you" and "go") and an occasional adopted country twang; she was devoted to the sanctity of written melody line; she was never in the least bit sharp or flat, other than in those rare instances in which the song called for it. Given all that, even detractors (and there are quite a few) who might not think those attributes make for a great singer have to agree that as a vocalist there has rarely if ever been one quite like her, and that like all the greatest singers, her voice is instantly recognizable.

What is *not* instantly recognizable to many people were all the business formalities, personnel clashes, strategic controversies, corporate battles, market forces, unexpected inconveniences, inopportune influences, and other perfectly normal roadblocks (normal for that industry, at least) that helped shape the Carpenters and their career. Karen was not just a gifted singer who happened to have a talented brother who knew how to select and arrange the songs that would make the two of them famous. She was also an active member of the Carpenters organization, involved in many decisions, both artistic and otherwise. If there was a creative difference between Richard and Karen, which sometimes there were, Karen was strong and confident enough to assert her opinion. Lyricist John Bettis recalled hearing a number of loud arguments between the siblings having to do with the direction in which a song was going. They admitted as much to newscaster Jerry Dunphy during a TV interview, recalling an argument over an arrangement. Richard called it a real "dilly" of a fight, and Karen said that in retrospect it was very funny, but that "It wasn't funny then!"

An occasional disagreement notwithstanding, she was known as a hardworking, dedicated professional who, along with her brother, got the job done and made the recording atmosphere one that her fellow professionals appreciated. Many people have stated that it was thrilling to be part of the Carpenters' studio experience. It is just another piece of testimony—one of hundreds in the world of entertainment—that someone can be deeply troubled and seriously flawed, as Karen was, yet still create something impressive, as she did.

Pam Zeitler, lead singer of The Carpenters Tribute Show, meets many people while touring who offer thoughts and comments about the ill-fated vocalist, and a majority of them, she says, aren't even interested in the troubles and the flaws; they relegate their comments to the music that Karen made and not the personal details that contributed to the eventual silence. "Most of us know she had a lot of problems," Zeitler says, "but I haven't really run into too many people who believe that her problems were any deeper than trying to be someone other than Richard's sister."

Karen *was* someone other than Richard's sister, but who knows if she would have been as compelling today, as a subject more than a singer, had the outcome been different. She may have been a pop star who was loved and admired deeply, but she may not have been scrutinized and worshipped as much as she is. The singularity of her voice, however, along with the almost impenetrable nature of her character, add to the mystique for those who cannot help but wonder about what was and what could have been.

As 1982 came slowly to a close, Karen's progress with the anorexia specialist she had selected was also proving to be exceedingly slow, traceable not necessarily to the treatment itself but to her apparent lack of sincerity in conceding and dealing with the problem in the first place. Karen was still living in New York City that fall, but after accepting the fact that she felt unwell, drained and confused—and recognizing that her heart was beating irregularly—she checked into Manhattan's Lennox Hill Hospital, where she was fed intravenously and carefully monitored. She also had a cardiology procedure to address the fatigue and heartbeat issues. There was complication: the surgeon inadvertently punctured one of her lungs. Karen was discharged in early November, visited her therapist one last time to say goodbye, then flew home to California.

In mid-December, back in California, she sang for a group of children at the Buckley School in Sherman Oaks, a school attended by her two godchildren, the twins of a close friend. That was her last performance. She would never sing in public or in a recording studio again. The voice of an incomparable talent, a spirited and puzzling woman-child, an American sweetheart, a lighthearted soul with a perpetually heavy heart, a very funny and lonely clown, was silenced. Not completely, though: fans who can never get enough know that there are many ways, and plenty of opportunities, to always hear the sounds of yesterday once more.

Selected Bibliography

Altschuler Glenn, *All Shook Up: How Rock 'n Roll Changed America*, Oxford, Oxford University Press, 2004.

Bacharach, Burt, *Anyone Who Had a Heart*, New York, HarperCollins, 2013.

Bego, Mark, *Billy Joel, the Biography*, New York, Thunder's Mouth Press, 2007.

Bogdenov, Vladimir; Woodstra, Chris; Erlewine, Stephen Thomas, editors, *All Music Guide, 4th Edition*, San Francisco, Backbeat Books, 2001.

Browne, David, *Fire & Rain: The Beatles, Simon & Garfunkel, James Taylor, CSNY and the Lost Story of 1970*, Cambridge, MA, Da Capo Press, 2011.

Butler, Patricia, *Barry Manilow, The Biography*, London, Omnibus Press, 2001.

Coleman, Ray, *The Carpenters: The Untold Story*, New York, HarperCollins, 1994.

Denver, John, *John Denver: Take Me Home*, New York, Random House, 1994.

Ewbank, Tim, *Olivia: The Biography of Olivia Newton-John*, London, Piatkus Books, 2006.

Eyman, Scott, *John Wayne: The Life and Legend*, New York, Simon & Schuster, 2014.

King, Carole, *A Natural Woman*, New York, Grand Central Publishing, 2012.

Levenkron, Steven, *Anatomy of Anorexia*, New York, W.W. Norton, 2001.

Levenkron, Steven, *The Best Little Girl in the World*, Chicago, Contemporary Books, 1978.

Maguire, James, *Impresario: The Life and Times of Ed Sullivan*, New York, Billboard Books, 2006.

Murray, Anne, *Anne Murray: All of Me*, Toronto, Vintage, 2010.

Perlstein, Rick, *Nixonland: The Rise of a President and the Fracturing of America*, New York, Scribner, 2009.

Ramone, Phil, *Making Records: The Scenes Behind the Music*, New York, Hyperion, 2007.

Rogers, Kenny, *Luck, or Something Like It: A Memoir*, New York, William Morrow, 2013.

Sedaka, Neil, *Neil Sedaka: Rock 'n Roll Survivor: The Inside Story of His Incredible Comeback*, London, Jawbone Press, 2013.

Schmidt, Randy, *Little Girl Blue: The Life of Karen Carpenter*, Chicago, Chicago Review Press, 2010.

Weintraub, Jerry & Cohen, Rich, *When I Stop Talking, You'll Know I'm Dead: Useful Stories from a Persuasive Man*, New York, Twelve, 2010.

Approximately 80 newspaper and magazine articles were consulted during the research for this book. The following provided some of the more vital and constructive information that was used:

The Los Angeles Times, Paul Grein (November 1989), Jean Rosenbluth (October 1996).

The New York Times, Rob Hoerburger (October 6, 1996).

People Weekly, Robert Windeler, "Karen and Richard Carpenter Aren't at the Top of the World: They Need to Be in Love" (August 2, 1976), Eric Levin, "...A Troubled Soul" (February 21, 1983), Richard Carpenter, "A Brother Remembers" (November 21, 1983).

Rolling Stone, Tom Nolan, "Up From Downey" (July 4, 1974), "A Song for You" (October 12, 1972), and Stephen Holden, "Carpenters: A Song for You" (October 12, 1972).

In addition to these books, magazines and newspapers, about three dozen websites, documentaries, and radio programs were of great value to the effort, notably:

Autopsy: The Last Hours of Karen Carpenter (ITV Studios, UK).

Close to You: Remembering the Carpenters (PBS)

A Current Affair.

CDBaby.com.

The Download, Chris May, Palm Springs.

Good Morning America.

I Love the 70s (VHI)

IMDB.com.

LeadSister.com.

Living Famously: Karen Carpenter (BBC).

TheMostBeautifulvoice.com.

Onamrecords.com.

Only Yesterday: The Carpenters' Story (BBC).

RichardandKarenCarpenter.com.

Songfacts.com

Thebacklot.com.

Notes

Please refer to the Bibliography and Acknowledgements pages for information on all of the sources used to compile this book both through personal interviews and from previously published or broadcast sources. While the sources number in the dozens, the following provided the most relevant historical and chronological foundation blocks upon which this literary excursion and assessment was built: Randy Schmidt's *Little Girl Blue: The Life of Karen Carpenter*, Ray Coleman's *The Carpenters: The Untold Story*, Tom Nolan's *Rolling Stone* article from July 1974, Paul Grein's *Los Angeles Times* article of November 1989, Chris May's series of interviews on *The Download*, the Richardandkarencarpenter. com website, the PBS documentary *Close to You: Remembering the Carpenters*, and the personal interviews conducted with Hal Blaine, Doug Strawn, and several former A&M employees. Direct quotes are always attributed within the text; sources of many indirect quotes or other factual stories and anecdotes that are not directly attributed in the text are noted below, except for those instances in which multiple research sources shared the same quotes and anecdotes.

Innocence and Melancholia

Peter O'Toole and Petula Clark: Coleman: The Carpenters: The Untold Story
Listening to her voice and the pitch: The Download

Teeny Grandmas and Burly Bikers

If I Were a Carpenter... sold extremely well: Jon Konjoyan
Madonna's 1993 single, "Rain": A&M Corner
Karen Carpenter had the clearest, purest voice: Songfacts.com

The Impact and the Crush

Karen was known to drum on whatever surfaces: Richardandkarencarpenter.com
Osborn told an interviewer... he was the one: Close to You: Remembering the Carpenters

Wow, what about her: Close to You: Remembering the Carpenters
The first was Uni... the second, White Whale: Coleman: The
Carpenters: The Untold Story
It was love at first hear: Close to You: Remembering the Carpenters

The Girl Behind the Drums

Her weight dropped to 91 pounds: Richardandkarencarpenter.com
When she was 17 a doctor recommended: Schmidt: Little Girl Blue
At one time she embarked on a rigorous exercise program:
Richardandkarencarpenter.com
Karen read Levenkron's 1978 novel: Schmidt: Little Girl Blue
Both Paul Williams and Petula Clark commented: Close to You:
Remembering the Carpenters
Dragon Lady: Schmidt: Little Girl Blue
Karen... helped set up breakfast: Schmidt: Little Girl Blue

Goody Four-Shoes

The remaining copies of the original Offering: onamrecords.com
I really don't think they knew exactly how: Close to You: Remembering
the Carpenters
When we first did TV early in our careers: Carl Goldman interview,
FM100
John Denver... called Weintraub: John Denver: Take Me Home
ABC was not happy with Music, Music, Music: Close to You:
Remembering the Carpenters
Richard and Karen never discounted: Doug Haverty

The Boss

Richard admitted to feeling a little bit overlooked: Paul Grein, *Los
Angeles Times*
Guitarist Russell Javors told a Billy Joel biographer: Bego, *Billy Joel,
the Biography*
Javors... once recalled he had read: Bego, *Billy Joel, the Biography*
John Bettis said that when Richard listened: The Download
You know why the album was shelved: The Download

Harmless Oblivion

Richard has stated that his Quaalude addiction: Richardandkarencarpenter.com
Richard... said he'd be more than willing to turn: Richardandkarencarpenter.com
Christmas Portrait... eventually passing more than: Richardandkarencarpenter.com
Richard once referred to Christmas Portrait as: Richardandkarencarpenter.com

Mrs. Karen Something-or-other

It has long been rumored that Richard sometimes sabotaged: Schmidt: Little Girl Blue
Karen liked Barry: Butler: Barry Manilow, The Biography
Liberty DeVitto has admitted that he fell in love: Schmidt: Little Girl Blue
One young man attending a Carpenters concert: Nolan: Rolling Stone
Several unsolicited engagement rings: Jerry Dunphy Visits
Karen decided that the father of: Schmidt: Little Girl Blue
Burris was promised: Schmidt: Little Girl Blue

All Shook Up

Kenny Rogers remembers that Karen sang: Rogers: Luck of Something Like It
Daugherty sued the label: Coleman: The Carpenters: The Untold Story

New and Old Horizons

Had it mixed and released just days: Richardandkarencarpenter.com
Largest grossing musical tour in Japanese history: IMDB

The End of Romance

Karen apologized to her family: Schmidt: Little Girl Blue
There were no bruises on her body: Autopsy: The Last Hours of Karen Carpenter
Her own daughter: Ewbank: Olivia, the Biography

When Time Was All He Had

It's sad to say, but there hasn't been nearly: The Download

Music, Music, Music

Karen speculated that with harder rock: Carl Goldman interview, FM100
Robert Christgau called Karen's voice: Robertchristgau.com

Postscript

Lyricist John Bettis recalled hearing: The Download
She also had a cardiology procedure: Coleman: The Carpenters, The Untold Story

Index

About the Author

Photo by Megan Gagliardi

Joel Samberg's previous book for BearManor Media was *Grandpa Had a Long One: Personal Notes on the Life, Career & Legacy of Benny Bell.* While Benny Bell's daughter-in-law (Joel's mother) may have despised the title, his fans enjoyed the book, which led to Joel's featured appearances in several magazine articles and on many radio programs, as well as in an upcoming documentary about Dr. Demento. Joel's own articles and essays have been published in *New York Times*, the *New York Daily News*, *New Jersey Monthly*, *Hartford Magazine*, *New Haven Magazine*, *Moment Magazine*, and many other publications. Two of his plays, *Six Tens from a Fifty* and *The Ballad of Bobby Blue*, were performed in New York and Connecticut, respectively. In 2013, his report on the 30th anniversary of the death of Karen Carpenter was heard on NPR's *All Things Considered.*

Joel can be reached at JoelSamberg@gmail.com. His website is http://JoeltheWriter.com.

CPSIA information can be obtained
at www.ICGtesting.com
Printed in the USA
LVOW04s0320280316

481029LV00017B/157/P